Shy Ghosts Dancing

Dark Tales from Southeast Alaska

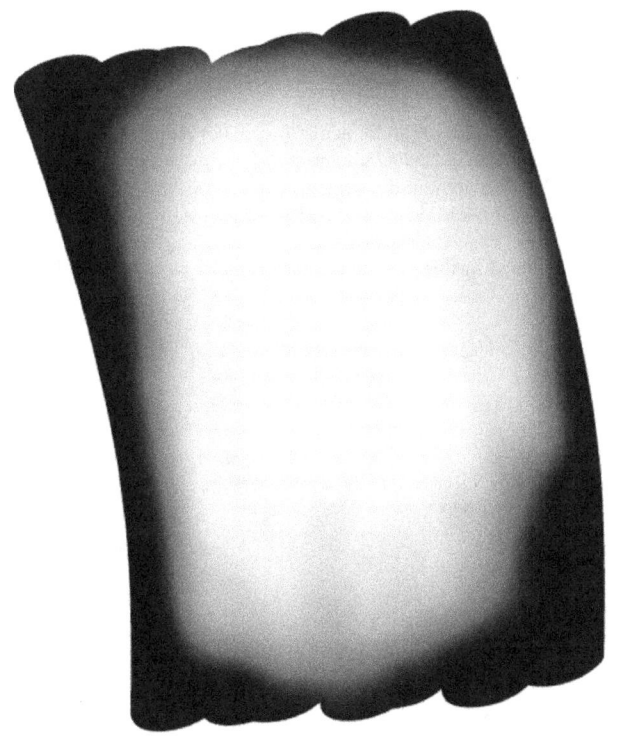

Yeldagalga Publications LLC, Haines Alaska

Shy Ghosts Dancing: Dark Tales from Southeast Alaska

The stories contained in this volume are fictional. No character should be construed to represent any real persons, alive or dead.

Published 2010 by Yeldagalga Publications LLC
PO Box 1316
Haines, AK 99827-1316
www.Yeldagalga.com

ISBN: 1612240003
EAN-13: 978-1-61224-000-8

Printed in the United States of America

Cover and interior design by Mark A. Zeiger
Artwork by Mark A. Zeiger, "Shy Ghosts Dancing," 2010

First Edition

This title is also available in e-book versions for Kindle and other electronic readers.

Shy Ghosts Dancing

Dark Tales from Southeast Alaska

Mark A. Zeiger

For my loves, Michelle and Aly.
Don't be afraid of the dark!

And in memory of my mother,
Gertrude Mae Holabird Zeiger
(1933 – 1998)

CONTENTS

FOREWORD

The region of Alaska known as Southeast or "The Panhandle" stretches from the state's southern border on Dixon Entrance south of Ketchikan to the vicinity of Yakutat in the northwest. Dominated by the Alexander Archipelago, a chain of mountainous islands that form the "Inside Passage," a relatively protected sea route, this heavily forested and rain swept land possesses great natural beauty and more than its share of mystery.

There's something about Southeast Alaska—a quality of light, an uncertainty of perspective and scale, or perhaps merely the way the forest grows that creates an astounding optical ambivalence. This often leads a person to stare steadfastly at an object, vainly trying to divine its true shape and identity from appearance alone—attempting to decode the sensory information offered, only to eventually, perhaps belatedly, discover its true nature. It might be a tangle of "witch's hair" moss hanging on a berry bush, a gnarled tree, or pattern of lichen on rock. The expected becomes the unexpected in an instant that is often followed by relief, as the seemingly dangerous proves to be mundane. Occasionally, that instant jars one from complacency, as the seemingly mundane proves dangerous.

I like writing that incorporates this mysterious atmosphere on some level. I've found hints of it in the works of a wide range of authors: Nick Jans, Barrett Willoughby, John Straley, Ferenc Máté, and Richard Nelson, but none of these wrote particularly dark or horror fiction. I couldn't find exactly the kind of recreational reading I sought, so I eventually decided to write my own.

Only one of the following tales lacks an Alaskan connection. Even so, it too includes themes drawn from my life in Alaska. Most of them strive to capture the atmosphere I've described in one way or another.

I've written fiction ever since I learned to write. As an adult I became interested in getting published. I knew it would be a long shot—the publishing world is neither welcoming nor kind to new writers. I aspired to, but certainly didn't expect to make a living at it.

I submitted my work, ranging from micro presses to major publications from 1994 to 1998. I sold two stories; one appeared in print; the other magazine folded before the story appeared. Not a bad start, but life intervened, partially because of the writing itself.

My wife, Michelle, told me that if we ever moved to a cabin in the woods, I could write full time. We liked that idea, and for a variety of reasons, began to plan ways to do it. We settled on building a live-aboard sailboat, as my brother and his wife had done. Building sailboats occupied my free time and most of my creative energy; the stories languished, mostly ignored, on my computer.

Since then, the printing world has changed. Web logs—"blogs"—have allowed writers like me access to an audience. Print on demand publishing is coming into its own. Aspiring writers can present their work to the public without the mediation or approval of publishers.

My world changed as well. My family now lives on a semi-remote "homestead" or smallholding, featuring a little log cabin on the forested shore of Alaska's Lynn Canal. Off the grid, subsistence living keeps us very busy, but I find time to write, posting essays about our life on the family's Web site and blog at AKZeigers.com. We hope to write a memoir of our life here one day.

In summer 2010, my older brother asked what I'd done with the stories I'd written, and suggested publishing them on demand as a new "micro income" to help sustain us here. The result is this book.

I've included a section at the end of the book that provides additional information on the stories—their origins or inspirations, personal thoughts about them, and more. I like this sort of trivia from authors I read, yet I can never decide whether I want to know the details *before* I've read the story, or *after*. I'll leave that up to you. The information's there if and when you want it.

So, here's my collection of stories: *Shy Ghosts Dancing: Dark Tales from Southeast Alaska.* As my Aunt Gail suggests, read it "next to a roaring fire, covered with a warm blanket, a cup of Russian tea in one hand and a big stick in the other."

SHY GHOSTS DANCING

The first night Dora and Vaughan camped on Admiralty Island, known as "Fortress of the Brown Bears," northern lights appeared in the sky.

It started faintly, indistinct appearances here and there, hesitating above the mountains across the water toward the north. The two young people held their breaths, watching shafts of light form against the darkness. Dora chuckled, observing how she and her companion kept still as if afraid to frighten it away.

"It's so tentative, I'm worried it'll see us and leave," she whispered, "It's like watching shy ghosts dancing!"

Vaughan wanted to call that poetic, but remained still. As if growing bolder, the aurora swelled until the sky filled with whipping, swirling sheets of luminescence. Dora rose from her seat by the fire and wandered down the beach, craning her neck to see.

It was then, while Vaughan sat alone, that the aurora borealis spoke to him for the first time, telling him Dora's terrible secret.

Vaughan had been surprised when Dora invited him to go bear hunting. Some Juneau hunters called her the best woman bear hunter around. Others called her the best bear hunter around, period. Her invitation singled Vaughan out from among several young men, all ardently in love, who continually vied for the young woman's attention.

"You and I ought to go bear hunting," she remarked one night. The other guys at their bar table responded enthusiastically, hoping the offer included them. She looked directly at Vaughan, focusing solely on him until he replied.

"Anytime, anywhere!" was all his wit could muster as Dora's intense brown eyes absorbed him. A classic Native beauty, her jet-black hair shone long and straight between well-muscled shoulder blades. Her jeans and body suit clung to every curve. Its scooped neck showcased her cleavage, prompting the two men on either side to tilt their heads awkwardly for a peek while sipping their beers. Vaughan felt the envious glances his friends gave him. Dora never invited anyone to go hunting. She always responded to offers with her favorite saying.

"Tarzan hunts best alone," she'd smile, so disarmingly no offense could be taken. Yet, the decision remained firm.

Dora smiled now, holding Vaughan's gaze, refusing to include the rest of the company with a glance around the table. One of her more aggressive suitors, Charlie Dock, objected.

"I thought Tarzan hunts best alone." It sounded more petulant than he intended; Dora punished him with a look.

"You're drinking too much, Charlie," she said. "You better give me that beer you ordered."

Vaughan had done very little hunting, and had never hunted bear. He was a camper and a photographer. He often tracked bear, but had no idea if he did it correctly. Judging from how few bears he had seen, he suspected he didn't. He told Dora as much, once the others left them alone. She just smiled.

"You don't need to know how. You'll be with me."

Vaughan chose his gear with care, trimming the list to barest essentials. Vaughan wanted to impress Dora, not earn her contempt.

As they loaded Dora's skiff on the day of their departure, Dora plucked his rolled tent from the pile of gear.

"May as well leave this in your truck," she told him. "Mine's plenty big enough for the two of us."

The day was warm for mid-September. By the time they reached the chosen beach on Admiralty Island, unloaded the skiff and pitched the tent, they were both heated.

"Let's swim," Dora said. She kicked off her boots and socks, then pulled her shirt over her head as she walked to the water. Vaughan stumbled down the cobble beach, eyes riveted on Dora with eager discomfort as her layers of clothing stripped away. She tossed her panties carelessly over her shoulder as the water rose to her firm, dark posterior. With a dive that revealed her most private places for the briefest instant, she disappeared beneath the surface. Hastily shucking his clothes, Vaughan followed.

The cold water shriveled him and took his breath, but he struggled to make a good show. When he ventured deep enough that his feet no longer touched bottom, he felt a silken rush up his front as Dora surfaced in his arms.

"Yow!" she squealed, whipping sheets of water from her hair and throwing her arms around his neck. "It's cold!" Vaughan felt nothing but her smooth skin against his, its gentle warmth searing in contrast to the frigid ocean. Leaning forward as if to kiss him, Dora ducked him under water instead. He shouted and thrashed after her as she sped away from him with graceful, even strokes.

As pleasant as the embrace had been, for all its momentary sexual tension, Vaughan realized Dora had not necessarily extended an invitation. She was playing. The moment had an unmistakable innocence to it.

Accepting this, he surrendered to her exuberance, participating willingly without attempting to push their activity further. They enjoyed frolicking nude in the icy water, and left it at that. Still, the memory kept Vaughan far warmer than he otherwise would have felt when evening cooled.

They lapsed into satisfied silence after dinner, enjoying the coming night. The air softened. The forest hushed behind them. The fire popped and sighed at their feet. They inched casually closer, leaning in toward each other almost unconsciously. Neither felt a need to speak, until Dora noticed and remarked on the aurora borealis.

Now, as the young woman wandered slowly down the beach with her eyes turned heavenward, the northern lights spoke to Vaughan, telling him things he didn't want to hear.

The voices, and there were several, weren't entirely distinct. They crackled and whistled like a poorly tuned radio signal. Many people claim to hear noises coming from auroras. Vaughan recalled a frigid winter night from his boyhood when he thought he heard them sing like a high-tension wire.

"Do you hear that?" Vaughan called to Dora. She'd gone beyond earshot, or had become too absorbed by the spectacle to answer. Confused and a little frightened, he listened to what the voices had to say.

They told him Dora was a bear, disguising herself as human. They warned she had led him to *Kootznoowoo*, using the Tlingit name for Admiralty Island, to give him to the brown bears.

Vaughan tried to answer, feeling like he did when, waking from a dream, he would discover that his dream shout barely reached a whisper. He wanted to deny what they told him, but no words came. The northern lights, swirling and shimmering, answered as if he'd spoken.

"See for yourself," the voices said, then fell silent.

Later, the two curled together in their sleeping bags. Vaughan stayed awake for hours. His mind flitted back and forth from the thrill of the day's intimacy, and Dora's sweet, soft, goodnight kiss, to the ominous revelations from the voices in the sky.

He knew local Native tradition held that all animals possessed human forms, which they normally hid under coats of fur or feather. Had this idea, rattling around in his subconscious, melded with his memories of crackling northern lights, creating aural illusions? He found it impossible to believe the aurora had spoken to him, of course, or that Dora was a bear. He found it improbable that she wished him harm. Furthermore, he didn't *want* to believe any of it.

Finally, lulled by Dora's gentle breathing against his throat, he slept.

By the next day's end, Vaughan began to believe the voices.

He awoke to Dora's singing as she moved about camp. Her clear voice rang in the morning stillness, accompanied by distant cries of ravens and gulls, and the faint rushing of a nearby creek. Vaughan smiled. Dismissing the previous night's uncertainty, he enjoyed the music, savoring the aroma of camp coffee and wood smoke. He hurried outside, greeting Dora warmly as she tossed eggshells into the steaming coffee pot to settle the grounds. She dazzled him with a smile, wordlessly offering a tin plate of eggs and hash.

In the glorious morning, momentarily sunny, dramatic clouds to the southeast promised a return to the region's customary weather before noon. Without conferring, they both pulled out raingear as they prepared to hunt.

Dora led the way, hiking silently inland. They pressed through the forest's heavy undergrowth, picking across occasional muskeg bogs before passing into more open country. Crossing a wild meadow, they came to a place where the long grass lay crushed and broken on either side of a muddy track. Churned hollows in the path, many filled with water, showed where generations of brown bears had ambled through on their way to fish for salmon. Dora pointed, indicating a distant cloud of seagulls, their racket audible from where they stood. Vaughan nodded. The gulls scavenged the salmon run in a nearby creek. They would find bears there as well.

They paralleled the trail, keeping a few yards off the path until they reached a low rise. High grass hid them from the creek while allowing them a relatively clear view. The breeze blew fresh in their face, sending their scent back the way they had come. Dora crouched, motioning Vaughan to follow. Below them in the creek bed, Alaskan brown bears fished.

In Kootznoowoo National Monument hunting is strictly regulated, allowing the island's ursine inhabitants to live almost undisturbed. Experts' low population estimate is 1.7 brown bears for each square mile on the huge island, a stunning statistic when one sees the size of the creatures. Kodiak Island, far to the west, is famous for the biggest examples of earth's largest land carnivore. The "brownies" of Southeast Alaska are hardly less impressive. Vaughan and Dora counted five adult males, and one female with a pair of yearling cubs.

Vaughan selected an enormous bruin with blond ears. Forcing moisture into his parched mouth, he leveled his rifle.

Dora reached over and gently pressed downward on the barrel with her hand. Vaughan lowered it with a questioning look.

"Why don't you take some pictures?" she breathed, indicating the camera hanging from his shoulder. Vaughan nodded. He spent the next hour taking photographs, tense and sweating, expecting the soft click of his shutter to bring the beasts down on them. Adrenaline raced through his body until he became almost euphoric from fear.

The animals romped and stumbled after fish, splashing comically. Only occasionally would one or another betray the true speed and predatory grace their kind possess. Then a fat salmon would magically appear, clamped in furry jaws. Seagulls, ravens, and eagles tussled and squawked among the indifferent bears, snatching tidbits where they could.

While Vaughan photographed, Dora watched the animals, totally absorbed. Vaughan glanced at her once or twice. She looked like she wanted to be with them, snatching salmon from the stream and tearing red sides of flesh in her teeth. He had almost forgotten the voices from the previous night, but the intensity with which she watched the bears reminded him of their warning.

Finally, Vaughan packed his camera and raised his rifle.

"No," Dora said.

"What?" he whispered. She turned with a look that betrayed a wildness he had never seen before, a feral quality, as if she were as much a creature of this island as the bears.

"Let's not," she said. He stared at her a moment longer, then looked at the animal he had targeted. It had to be trophy-sized, he thought. With a quick glance back at the woman, he shook his head, raising the weapon again.

Dora yanked a handful of long grass, dislodging a clump of sod. Whipping it in a quick circle, she lobbed it through the air in a high, dirty arc. It thudded among the bears, scattering birds in all directions.

"No!" she shouted.

Vaughan gasped. The bears might ignore them, but if one were startled into attacking, it could easily close the gap between the stream and the rise in seconds.

Momentarily frozen, the great beasts suddenly reacted. The sow hustled her cubs up the far bank as if they were newborns rather than yearlings close to her size. Vaughan's blond and two others reared on stout hind legs to peer at the intruders. The nearest one dropped to all fours and charged. Vaughan's knees weakened, but he stood still, gambling his life that it was a bluff rush. The bear would probably stop well short of them for another look. Probably.

Dora stood beside him, holding his gun barrel toward the ground, refusing to let him raise it. Hers hung from her other hand, muzzle down. She began to back away slowly, pulling Vaughan after her. The charging male stopped a considerable distance from them, as Vaughan predicted. It reared up to watch their retreat. The sow peeped over the far rise, then almost sheepishly led her cubs back to the creek. The other bears soon lost interest, returning to the salmon.

Neither hunter spoke as they hiked back to camp. The rain came, churning up sweet, heavy, temperate rainforest fragrance, while making their progress slow and wet. It did nothing to improve Vaughan's mood.

"See for yourself," the aurora borealis had told him.

He replayed every incident in his mind, examining each detail. Dora seemed so wild, so natural. Her unashamed nudity, her eagerness to swim in the bone-chilling ocean, even her taciturn ways all appeared in ominous new light. She had led him to the bears, but had not let him shoot, the whole point of the trip. Insignificant details grew in importance as they slogged through mud and muskeg. Something was definitely not right about her. He still doubted the voices, but didn't realize he no longer doubted hearing them.

They reached camp and stowed their gear. Vaughan stood, hands in pockets, accusing her with his stare.

"What happened back there?" he finally asked.

"It wasn't right," Dora shrugged. "Things are better left undone until they feel right." She raised her eyes to pin him with her gaze. "Everything happens when it's supposed to." She removed her wool coat. Grabbing the waist of her shirt, she began to pull it off. Vaughan stood stunned. She stopped and looked at him, her shirt hem level with her breasts, the bottoms of which peeped from beneath her fingers.

"Are you swimming?" she asked. It took Vaughan a moment to shift gears before shaking his head. She shrugged again, stripped, grabbed a bar of soap, and walked calmly through pouring rain to the water.

Vaughan stomped around the beach in a huff, but paused often to watch Dora. She stood waist-deep in the gentle surf, singing in her clear voice. She bathed luxuriantly, lathering her long, shapely arms, lovely breasts, and shoulders. Vaughan smoldered over losing the bear, about misunderstanding her in camp, about refusing her invitation to join her, naked, in the water. Doubt and desire tormented him. The voices from the northern lights seemed to return inside his head, crackling out their warning once again.

A whoop and a large splash startled him from his brooding. Dora rushed from the water, dragging a good-sized salmon by its gill slits.

"Look at this!" she cried.

"How did you do that?" he called in surprise.

"I just caught it," she laughed. "It was easy! Just like the bears, except I didn't use my teeth!"

When Vaughan reached camp, Dora was squatting naked by the fire, cleaning the fish. She dangled a strip of red meat over her upturned face and lowered it into her mouth with great relish. Seeing Vaughan's look, she grinned.

"Sushi," she said. He shook his head and turned away, thinking of the brown bears stripping sides off the salmon they caught.

The wind shifted, becoming northerly. Dora sniffed the air, predicting clear skies. She chunked the salmon, then returned to the water for an armload of kelp. She wrapped salmon pieces in the slippery fronds, placing them in aluminum foil to steam in the campfire coals. She rubbed herself dry in the fire's warmth, then dressed, to Vaughan's abashed relief and disappointment.

They ate in silence, but one so companionable on Dora's part that Vaughan began to warm to her again, in spite of his fears. They watched as the sky cleared and stars appeared.

"Look, Vaughan," Dora said in a low voice, "the shy ghosts have come to dance again."

What had a moment before seemed only wisps of cloud lit by stars or firelight became the first tentative illuminations of aurora borealis. Soon the night sky filled, as it had before, with pin wheeling, rippling sheets of light.

"Do you hear that?" Vaughan asked cautiously. Dora briefly turned her gaze from the sky to him.

"What? Do you hear it crackling or something? People say it does, sometimes."

"You don't hear it?" he asked again. She shook her head. He immediately dropped the subject, reluctantly turning his attention to what the voices in the sky were saying.

As filmy apparitions undulated across the sky, the voices returned like transmissions from deep space. They warned him again that Dora was a bear in disguise, who planned to feed him to her people on the salmon creek.

Again Vaughan tried to shout, to ask the voices who they were, and how they knew the message they delivered. As before, his voice wouldn't respond.

Eventually, the night sky stilled.

Dora scooted nearer as Vaughan struggled to sort his thoughts. She smelled of soap, salt water, wood smoke, and warm woman. When they were shoulder-to-shoulder, she regarded him with a strange, secret smile, and nudged him hard. Vaughan felt his desire combat his fear of her, and lose ground.

"Do you want to turn in?" she asked. "We should get to the creek early tomorrow." He rose with her and followed like a captive to the tent.

They watched each other, each thinking private thoughts as Dora combed her raven hair, then adjusted her sleeping bag so the zipper opened toward Vaughan's. She removed her clothing and slid into the bag. Propped on one elbow, facing him as he lay on his back, she searched his expression for a moment. Finally, she sighed softly, as if she had found in his eyes the answer to an unasked question.

"Things will happen when they're supposed to, Vaughan Jacobs," she said, softly. She slid her hand into his shirt, leaning close to kiss his firmly set lips. Then, with a smile that held, he thought, an ominous hint of sadness, she settled down in her sleeping bag.

Vaughan listened to her sleep, his blood running cold as she snored gently with a sound like the grumbling of the island's great bears. Exhausted, he drifted into nightmare-haunted sleep, convinced that in the morning he would die.

He had decided by the time they retraced their steps to the creek near sunrise. Vaughan slipped the safety off the rifle he carried. He tensed, ready to use it against the woman or any of her ursine family should they pounce unexpectedly.

Vaughan noticed large tracks mixed with their footprints from the day before. Apparently, a bear had tracked them from the creek, but the camp had not been disturbed in the night. He almost called Dora's attention to this, but remained silent. The fact she did not mention the sign only convinced him further of the danger he faced.

Inland meadows steamed in the warming day. The mist hid all kinds of horrors for Vaughan. Muffled sounds around them suggested giant bears stealing closer for the kill. The moist air and their steady hiking heated him till he swam in perspiration.

They found more bears at the creek than the previous day. The beasts squabbled and cuffed each other, vying for the best fishing stations. The blond-eared bear had returned to defend his spot. Vaughan arrived like a condemned man to the scaffold, resigned to his fate, yet wildly grasping at any and all avenues of escape. He immediately removed his gear to allow maximum mobility. He watched the bears while tracking Dora's movements beside him. She seemed uneasy as well, perhaps nervous about what she planned to do. Still, she said nothing, watching the bears with her rifle lowered.

"Why don't you do it?" he finally whispered, exasperated by suspense, willing an end to the situation.

"I'm waiting for the right moment," she replied.

She was always in control, just like her furry kin in the creek. No need for hurry, every move deliberate and sure, born of centuries as unchallenged monarchs of the island. Vaughan decided to force her to act, giving himself the decisive advantage.

He faced her, swinging the muzzle of his weapon level with her breasts.

"What are you doing?" she cried, forgetting the bears for an instant.

"I'm ending it!" he shouted, finger tightening on the trigger. Blood roared in his ears. His vision swam. He couldn't believe he was being forced to kill the woman he loved to save himself. He felt absorbed by Dora's beautiful, dark eyes, now open wide in terror.

Vaughan hesitated an instant longer, watching her stare through him, and, as if in slow motion, raise her own rifle. Ready, he acted more quickly, even as a blast of hot, stinking breath lashed the back of his head. The air near his right ear whistled, torn by the force of a giant paw closing with lethal intent. As two guns fired simultaneously, Vaughan watched, confused, as the ground swept crazily away from him.

◆ ◆ ◆ ◆ ◆

Evening had fallen by the time Dora finished. Even so, she boarded the skiff and turned it homeward, unwilling to remain another night on *Kootznoowoo*.

She felt distraught, unable to piece together or make sense of the day's events.

She tried to prepare for the ordeal ahead. She would arrive in Juneau late at night with a prize brown bear and a mutilated corpse in her skiff. There would be hard questions, and plenty that needed to be done.

The man she loved lay wrapped in a tarp in the skiff bottom, shattered by the bear she shot as it killed him. Her plans for a simple hunting trip and a chance to be alone with Vaughan to reveal her feelings for him had gone incredibly, inexplicably sour.

Dora had taken months to muster the courage to ask Vaughan on the hunt. She admired his gentleness, and his acceptance of her quiet ways. He seemed willing to give her the time she needed to reveal her love for him in her own manner. She thought he was letting her make the first move. Now, it was impossible to say what had motivated him, or what had caused him to turn on her.

Dora didn't want to believe that Vaughan meant to kill her when he died. She would never tell anyone, but if the blond-eared bear hadn't struck him as he pulled the trigger, spoiling Vaughan's pointblank shot, she too would be dead.

Things happened when they were supposed to, she believed, but what she supposed would happen was far different from this.

Dora steered toward the distant lights of Juneau. Above her, the aurora borealis faintly appeared, fading in and out of view like shy ghosts dancing.

WHACKING THE GROANER

Fog swirling on the dark surface of the cold north Pacific alternately hid and revealed a sodden, freezing boy. In shock, close to drowning, struggling to keep his head above water, Tyler Croft had just witnessed something thought to be extinct for some sixty-five million years. There's an old story told in Southeast Alaska. When the Russians came to the chain of islands they named the Alexander Archipelago, they marked areas significant to navigation with buoys. The story tells how the appearance of one of these markers caused great alarm among the Natives. A nearby village's bravest men canoed out to examine this strange object. They could make no sense of what they saw. One man raised a heavy war club and struck the buoy. The huge barrel boomed and reverberated, a noise so loud, so unexpected, and so strange to the men, that everyone in the canoe fainted dead away!

Now buoys and markers in a variety of shapes, sizes, and uses dot the treacherous Alaskan coast. Young Tyler Croft and his friends often fell asleep at night, or woke in the morning to the sound of a whistle buoy. Tyler's father, whose people came from New England, called these buoys "groaners."

Coastal folk whose lives and livelihoods depend on buoys would no more tamper with a buoy than you would a traffic light or power line. Tyler and his friend, Christopher, forgot or overlooked this important point one gray day in early September.

It began when Tyler told the story of the Natives' encounter with the Russian marker.

"...and they all dropped dead on the spot!" Tyler finished with a flourish much appreciated by his listener.

"Wow!" Christopher paused to think this over.

"What killed them?" he finally asked, feeling slightly foolish.

"What do you mean?" Tyler narrowed his eyes and cocked his head slightly to one side, an expression he hoped conveyed scorn.

"Well," Christopher hesitated, "was it the sound the buoy made? Did the vibration kill them, or what?"

Tyler's scorn vanished. It was his turn to think for a moment.

A sound intruded on the lull in their conversation: a low, mournful moan. It penetrated the thick fog to where they perched on a drift log at the edge of the Pacific. They both looked out over the water, knowing the

13

buoy they heard lay completely out of sight in the mist. They looked at each other.

They grinned.

Twenty minutes later they paddled through the fog in Tyler's family canoe, following the intermittent call of the groaner somewhere out in the channel. They carried little cargo, mostly snack food raided from home cupboards and a small emergency pack, included as a rule on any canoe outing. They also carried Christopher's prized, white ash baseball bat.

"Are you sure you can find it in this fog?" Christopher asked.

"I can find it. Look, it's right there!" Tyler dragged his paddle to slow the canoe, gliding gently up to the large, dark shape looming out of the mist.

Christopher glanced back at his friend for reassurance, then carefully rose, balancing himself against the gunwales. Once set, he raised his bat and took careful aim at the low, metal base that floated the marker in the channel. After a short pause, in which each boy steeled himself against the possibly lethal consequences of their action, Christopher swung the bat.

They judged the result to be quite satisfying. They had pounded on empty 55-gallon drums before, but this sounded twice as deep, twice as loud. The reverberation rattled their teeth, filling the air with sound. Neither of them died, nor even fainted. Christopher and Tyler grinned at each other.

"Do it again!" Tyler gushed.

"Naturally," drawled Christopher, hitching his pants like a Big League batter at the plate. He drew back and whacked the base of the buoy once more. This time, the impact coincided with the long, low whistle of the mechanism.

The combined tones delighted the boys. They giggled crazily, shaking the canoe.

"One more time!" Tyler shouted. "Wait for the whistle, and do it again, that was awesome!" Christopher measured his chance, then swung a third time. The buoy emitted a simultaneous boom and moan. Soon Christopher had established a rhythm, and struck the metal skin just as the next whistle began, creating an eerie vibration that shimmered across the water. Each tone elicited screams and wild laughter from the two boys.

"What was that?" Tyler asked suddenly, gripping the gunwales and peering seaward through the fog. Christopher concentrated on his timing, waiting for the next swing.

"What was *what?*" he asked, shrugging, not really listening for an answer.

"Something's out there," Tyler said as Christopher beat the buoy again. The edge in Tyler's voice caught Christopher's attention. As the tandem sounds rolled over the water, he turned to look at his friend. Immediately, he crouched in the canoe, seizing the gunwales himself.

"What do you see? Is it a whale?"

"I don't know; could be. Something big moved out there. It jiggled the boat, did you feel it?" Christopher shook his head, peering around.

"There!" Tyler exclaimed, pointing toward the open water at the sound of a deep, chuffing hiss. "Hear it spout?" His companion nodded, his whole being focused toward the sound's source. They barely heard the creature's misty exhalation above the dying sound of the big buoy.

Tense, excited, they crouched, listening and watching. Moments passed. The groaner gave forth half a dozen times as they waited. The boys slowly relaxed.

"Probably just went by," Tyler shrugged. "Dad says they can cruise for a long time underwater if they want to. Come on, bang that thing a couple more times." Christopher retrieved his bat and positioned himself, waiting for the next whistle. When it came, he swung, creating the odd sound again. The boys collapsed in fresh laughter.

Abruptly, something collided with the hull of the canoe somewhere amidships. Tyler threw himself down. Christopher lost his balance and joined his friend in the canoe bottom with a thump. The water around them roiled. Their craft abruptly lifted almost clear of the surface, then began to bump and shudder as it slowly settled. To Tyler, it felt like dragging a rough-cut handsaw slowly across the edge of a board. His mind's eye showed him a serrated back passing beneath the thin skin of their canoe. He opened his mouth to shout to Christopher, but an unbelievable sight stopped him.

On the far side of the groaner, the slate-colored water bulged and lightened. A streamlined form pushed up and up until the surface tension broke. The split water whitened and foamed around the force passing through it. Tyler's eyes widened, his mouth making a little 'O' of wonder, as a massive form twisted and rolled, chopping the water around it. The object seemed slick, yet pebbly or scaly. It appeared to be light, mossy green. Tyler's young mind processed sensory data, comparing, then discarding information, trying to comprehend what he saw. The idea that they were encountering a whale at extreme close range still held, although he could not see anything that would confirm that assumption. As the thing rolled, a huge, pale flipper hove above the surface of the water, wavered, and slapped down hard, drenching the boys as they trembled in their pitifully small canoe.

Tyler had seen humpback whales behave like this, lazily waving their impossibly long flippers. This flipper was not, he recognized even in his shocked state, a whale's. Stouter, more suggestive of a hand, this flipper had ridges beneath the green skin like long, fused fingers.

The strange creature suddenly flipped and dove, buffeting the canoe. Tyler scanned frantically, still trying to get a mental picture of the whole being as parts of it flashed past. It was incredibly fast, disappearing completely in an instant. The huge body displaced masses of water as it went, sending the canoe swinging wildly in a deep whirlpool until it rammed hard, broadside, against the groaner's base just as the buoy began emitting another low moan. Quite unintentionally, the groaner was whacked again, sending out the tandem vibration.

The water bulged and split more quickly this time, as a huge, sharp muzzle pushed out of the water. An immense, saurian form rose above them. Tyler saw an eyeball as big as his father's fist. Massive jaws opened, showing large, pointed teeth, and a gullet like a mineshaft. The creature rose farther in the air, then blasted the cowering children with a roar that perfectly mimicked the combined sound of the beaten buoy and its signal.

Tyler and Christopher instantly released the gunwales to mash their palms over their ears against the rush of sound. They grabbed for hand holds again as the great beast sank lower into the water, then turned and dashed the surface into spume as it dove.

Christopher's mouth worked rapidly, but it took a moment for Tyler to make sense of the words his friend chanted in a questioning singsong.

"Tylosaur? Kronosaur? Zeuglodon? Mososaur? Platecarpus? Tylosaur? Kronosaur...." The chant focused Tyler's thoughts, allowing him to consider what Christopher already had, and was trying to work through for himself.

The two boys loved prehistoric animals. They encountered imaginary dinosaurs often enough in their play. Had they just seen a real prehistoric sea creature—a mososaurus or something similar? They had heard the theories of the Loch Ness monster. They spent plenty of time discussing the reported monsters in their own state, of Lake Iliamna and Raspberry Strait, far to the northwest. They delighted in the possibility that undocumented survivors of prehistoric ages flourished in populations unconfirmed by science.

Tyler knew, but still could not accept, what they had encountered. He had played with his own toy mososaurus so often, so intently, had examined it from so many angles, that even now—animated and magnified far beyond the miniature—he recognized it. Only common sense slowed the revelation. Boyish fantasy couched in parascientific speculation was one thing. Actually confronting a real creature of this sort was another matter entirely.

They had no time to thoroughly consider the situation. The canoe, now half-full of water, still thrashed about. Tyler grabbed a paddle and worked to steady the craft, bawling at Christopher to bail. Christopher retrieved a coffee can floating in the wash and frantically scooped water from the canoe.

As Tyler struggled with his paddle, the canoe prow swung once more against the buoy float. It boomed in time with the next whistle. Before the sound faded, the behemoth returned. Rocketing straight out of the water, it rose high, throwing spray in all directions. The terrified children saw a gigantic saurian form, with huge oar-like flippers, a long, sharp, dragon's head, and a ridged fin cresting down the creature's back. As it ascended, it blasted their ears with its bellow, drowning out the groaner's fading vibration.

"It's a *mating call*," Tyler murmured. "The groaner called it—*we* called it!" The wave created by the massive bulk rising from the depths struck the canoe, knocking the prow into the air. Christopher flew from the boat, vanishing in the water with a pitifully small splash. Tyler screamed, clinging to the canoe as it bobbed in the chop. He tore his eyes away from the creature to search for his friend through the showering spray.

The mososaur settled heavily back into the water, regarding the metal buoy briefly. Suddenly, it swung its massive head, striking the marker with its long, tooth-filled jaw. The groaner's metal frame shrieked as it sped through the water, crashing against the canoe. With nothing to weigh it down other than a small boy in the stern, the canoe skipped and tumbled across the surface of the water. Tyler scrabbled for a handhold, gained it, but found no support. The next instant he surfaced in numbingly cold water, thrashing and spitting. His right hand still clung to the handhold he had grasped, the strap of the emergency pack his father insisted he carry in the canoe.

The creature, agitated now, swirled around the buoy in tight loops, battering it with its snout. It savaged the marker with its huge jaws, the long sharp teeth puncturing the support girders in several places, denting them deeply in others. Tyler washed this way and that, struggling to keep breathing as wave after wave from the thrashing beast doused him. Between gouts of seawater he searched for the canoe and for Christopher. The canoe appeared briefly once, flying through the air, launched by a sweep of the creature's huge tail. To Tyler's momentary relief, it was too far away to endanger him.

The pack in his hand grew heavy. Tyler's shock-fogged mind cleared for a second. He stopped struggling long enough to pull out a packet of flares before letting the pack sink. Freeing the pull chain of one flare caused him to lose the others. They may have floated away, he couldn't be sure. The boy raised the flare above his head, sinking as he did so. He pointed it skyward as well as he could, and yanked the chain, hoping he had managed to ignite the signal before it submerged. He felt brief heat on his hands, then painful cold as he slipped completely underwater. He immediately lowered his arms, putting his remaining strength into a stroke to bring his head back to the surface.

Fisting his eyes clear of salt water, Tyler saw the flare's glow far above. He had managed to ignite it, and send it high enough that it might be seen.

Looking around, he also saw the mososaur. It seemed to have calmed slightly. He located the monster just as it shot past the buoy, sending a new wall of force through the surrounding water. It seemed to focus on something ahead of it, making a lightning-fast extra lunge, then slowing and looping back toward the buoy. With a toss of its missile-shaped snout, it seemed to swallow. Tyler could barely think what had just happened, and didn't want to.

The creature turned toward Tyler. The boy shivered from the icy water, and from uncontrollable terror. The beast plowed to within twenty feet of the floating child, then veered off toward the buoy. Ramming with its head at incredible speed, the leviathan blasted the groaner off its moorings, sending it rushing through the water. Then the creature dove, ducking downward and flowing in a tightly curved hump of green skin and frilled crest that seemed to go on and on as Tyler watched. Finally, the tip of the long tail appeared, flicked, and vanished.

The canoe had disappeared. Tyler saw no trace of Christopher. Even the buoy was gone, leaving him submerged to his trembling chin in the suddenly flat calm, slate-colored water. The fog settled around him, cloaking him in silence.

A sudden thought robbed Tyler of his momentary, overwhelming relief. He remembered the creature's freight train rush out of the deep. He wondered if another one might be imminent, this time from directly below, with those huge jaws and that mineshaft gullet opened wide to gobble him up. In that instant Tyler recalled that fossil remains revealed that mososaurs possessed a second row of teeth, just forward of the throat at the back of the jaws. This recollection overshadowed everything he'd just experienced.

He felt a vibration in the water around him, starting faint and growing stronger. He struck out, dog paddling furiously to get away, only to realize he had nothing to swim for other than the far-distant beach. In which direction that lay, he had no clue.

The vibration grew louder, until it became a churning in the water. Tyler breathed again the moment he realized it was a boat motor. Someone had seen his flare, and sped to the rescue.

But would it be in time? Was the mososaur below him, just now turning to begin a long, lethal ascent? He gathered his remaining strength and yelled, waving his arms frantically over his head.

Hypothermic, he managed only a faint cry, like a lost seal pup. The dense, surrounding fog immediately absorbed the noise, hushing and spiriting it away with seemingly malicious intent. He called again, raising the volume a bit through tremendous effort, then slumped, feeling his water-soaked clothing begin to pull him under.

The Coast Guard auxiliary vessel, *Rhiannon II*, appeared in the fog. A deckhand keeping careful watch in the bow bellowed a warning. The skipper slowed the boat, guiding it expertly past the child. Seconds later, Tyler felt strong hands pluck him from the water.

Immediately he became the helpless center of a flurry of business. They roughly hustled him about as they worked to revive and warm him, until he began to feel he hadn't been rescued at all, but still floated at the mercy of the behemoth.

"What's he saying?" Tyler heard through the scraping, bustling chatter. He didn't realize until then that he was saying anything.

"He's saying 'mososaur' over and over," another voice said.

"Moso what?"

"It's a type of dinosaur," a third voice said.

"You gotta be kidding..." a woman started.

"I don't get it," the first one said, uncertainly. Tyler's vision cleared to show a circle of faces hovering above him. They showed concern, confusion, and a hint of fear. One man glanced over his shoulder, perhaps wondering what secret lurked, unknown, in the surrounding dark water.

"Let's get him to the hospital," one said. "He's delirious. Get something warm into him now!" They bundled Tyler in wool blankets, then bore him into the flying bridge. As he faded into exhausted sleep, Tyler followed the skipper's gaze across the mysterious, black surface of what he had considered, only hours ago, to be familiar waters.

THE BLOOFER LADY

...My sister, Jewel Trickney, gets my house, the car, and my rifles. Everything else goes to Bob Valarial.

Tobias Sparkes started as he read this, having mused an instant before, that people who wrote in U.S. Forest Service cabin journals sometimes composed as if they were writing their last will and testament.

Sparkes had read the journals in nearly every U.S.F.S. cabin in Southeast Alaska. Basically intended to provide information about the cabin—available fuel and water, damage, presence of wildlife, and outhouse conditions—the journals have become a sort of yearbook in which members of the camping fraternity scribble their thoughts, feelings, and memories of their stay. Sparkes found them fascinating. No matter how brief his stay, he always made time to read the cabin journal.

In them he found everything—speeches, hopelessly obscure inside jokes, disjointed political rants, and idiotic, chemically induced meanderings. He found heartwarming stories of budding romance, newlyweds, and anniversary celebrations. He found inscriptions from foreign visitors, and from people he knew. He read hilarious stories of comic mishaps, cooking adventures gone awry, misidentified wildlife, and outlandish fiction. He read poetry, usually inspired by the cabin's setting or view, and scripture from Bible, Koran, and Talmud. Illustrations occasionally decorated the margins, from children's scribbles to beautifully executed studies by known and unknown artists. Some people carefully pressed wildflowers from nearby meadows between the pages. Quite often he skipped a paragraph or two, recognizing his own hurried scrawl from past visits.

He once compared the journals to folklore or family history, in that they connected readers with those who had come before. Privately, he depended on them. They kept him sane when wind and rain drove him to the shelter of fire and candlelight. He found much of what he read unbelievable, some of it troubling, but none more so than the series of entries he found at Butler Cabin.

Sparkes had eagerly anticipated his turn at the newly built cabin. Most stays are limited to three days, but cabins that are salt water accessible, like Butler, could be reserved for a whole week.

"Water accessible" can be misleading. Reaching the cabin required a hike of some eight steep miles from tidewater to the lovely alpine meadow where the shelter nestled, in dramatic proximity to Butler Glacier, for which it had been named.

Sparkes reserved a week in January, planning to reach the cabin by cross-country ski. As often happens, unpredictable Alaskan weather adjusted his plans. A January thaw removed much of the snow. He hiked most of the way, his skis strapped to his pack, sinking to his kneecaps in slushy, rotten snow and muskeg. The thaw laid bare the plank walkway, a trail type used throughout the region to preserve the delicate muskeg ecology.

He enjoyed the planking in summer, when it crossed meadows bursting with heather, shooting star, chocolate lily, fly-catching sundews, lupine, and Alaska cotton. The silvered planks, nailed to their improbable piles of supports, meandering through this landscape, reminded him of Dr. Seuss illustrations. He half-expected to encounter a Sneetch as he hiked, or perhaps, toward evening, a pair of pale green pants with nobody inside 'em! In winter, the plank trails became useless, buried by snow. Uncovered, they could be dangerous, coated with sheets of ice that broke and sledded on slick, wet wood. Hikers risked injuries ranging from skinned knees to broken legs on these paths.

Still, the unseasonably warm breeze in Sparkes's face refreshed and invigorated him. For safety's sake he took his time, delaying his planned arrival at Butler cabin by several hours.

Dark fell an hour before he reached his destination. Rain began fifteen minutes later. Sparkes had lived in Alaska all his life. He thought little of rain, except when it fell as it did that day, in relentless, icy waves, soaking him through his wool sweater until his shoulders ached with cold. To his great relief, the little cabin finally appeared in the gloom. Soon he was inside, stripped of wet clothing, admiring the curling steam rising around him, coaxed by a warming woodstove.

Later, his gear stowed, his gun oiled, his body fed, Sparkes scooted the rough-hewn table across the room from the southeast window to the northwest. This would offer a daylight view of the glacier if the weather cleared. Seating himself and adjusting the lantern, he reached for the cabin journal.

Paging through the few entries, reading a line here and there, he smiled at his last will and testament thought, just as his eye caught the bequeathing line. Fighting the urge to continue from there, Sparkes turned back to the boldly stroked manuscript's beginning, and began to read:

November 12, 1995: Made good time on the hike. Got to the cabin just before sunset and snowfall—thanks, Karen and Peter, for all the split wood! Got settled and fed quickly. The bottle of wine proved worth the extra weight. It warmed me as I sat watching the snow fall, adding to the three feet already on the ground. I moved the table to the southeast window, since it's closer to the stove. I'll move it back when it clears off or I leave, whichever comes first.

November 13: Slept uneasily last night. I had a strange feeling I wasn't alone. Don't know why.

Hunted deer on the ridge all day. No luck. I'll try again tomorrow. The snow never really let up. Waist deep in places. I got soaked and sore, but I'm drying out by the stove now, feeling much better. Funny though, the feeling I had last night came back when the sun set—I sense someone standing behind me, as if waiting to catch my attention. I'm looking over my shoulder a lot! Saw movement at the edge of the clearing outside the southeast window. Thought it might be deer, but I never saw any, even though I kept close watch until well after midnight.

November 14: Snow is falling hard again. I'll get snowed in if I don't leave. The deer must have already been driven down mountain by the weather. I won't get anything up here. I'll head out tomorrow.

Something is definitely moving at the edge of the clearing. It's pale, and blends in with the snow around it. It might be snow falling off the boughs, but I don't see branches springing up after losing the weight.

November 15: Snowed in. I tried to hike out, but gave up before I'd made a half-mile from the cabin. It's chest deep most places now, deeper in spots. No matter. I've got the cabin for a week. There's plenty of food, water, and firewood. Things will probably change by the end of the week if not before. I'll be out of wine by then, though. Cheers!

November 16: Something weird is going on! Last night I sat at the window again, watching the snow fall. I swear I saw a person out there! It looked like a woman with long hair that was whipped around by the wind. She stood still or moved back and forth a few paces. She wore a white poncho or robe, or maybe even a sheet. I watched her for a few minutes, but just as I decided to go out on the porch, she turned and walked into the woods. I called to her, but the wind had picked up, and my voice didn't carry. I went to the edge of the clearing to look. I didn't see any marks, which wasn't too surprising since the snow fell so hard, but after I got back to the cabin, it occurred to me: the snow came up to my hips at the edge of the clearing. The person I saw stood _above_ the snow. I could even see her feet!

This morning I looked again. All my tracks got covered. The snow wasn't crusted at the edge of the clearing, either, so she couldn't have stood on top of it. I did have wine last night, but not enough to get drunk, even if I had finished the whole bottle. I don't know what to make of this.

November 17: She came back last night, right about sunset, which I could only guess at because the clouds have been so low, and the snow heavy all day. She appeared at the edge of the forest. I'm sure it's a young woman. She just stood at the tree line, watching the cabin, pacing a little now and then. It looked like she walked across the top of the snow, but I can't see how. Maybe there's a bench buried out there? Just like last night, she turned and walked into the woods just as I got up to go outside. Spooky.

November 18: I can't get out. I cut trail all day. Didn't even make it to the creek. Should have brought snowshoes. I'll have to stay until the weather changes. I admit, I'm kind of glad. I'm really curious about my strange "friend." I know who she is! She's the Bloofer Lady! Remember, from _Dracula?_ Not the movies, Stoker's book!

Later... The Bloofer Lady is back. As I'm writing this she stands at the clearing, barely visible in the lantern's glow. She seems to be staring right at me. I'm going to wave. She's beckoning to me! She just pulled her hair away from her face—she's beautiful!

<u>November 19</u>: *I hope she comes back tonight. She's all I thought about today. I thought she might be camped nearby, but now I don't think so. I went out onto the porch and called to her last night. She didn't answer, she just kept beckoning to me, smiling. What a smile! I was right, she <u>is</u> beautiful. I started to follow her, but when she disappeared into the forest I suddenly realized I was chest-deep in snow, wearing nothing but my long johns! I took about two hours getting warm and dry again. That was close.*

Later... The Bloofer Lady knows my name.

I am beginning to get seriously freaked out about this whole situation. She came to the edge of the clearing about an hour ago and started calling me. Her voice is like music—warm and low-pitched—but her lungs must be incredible, because I can hear her above the wind and the muffling snowfall. I covered the window, but I still hear her out there, calling me. I wonder why? I wonder who the hell she is?

<u>November 20</u>: *I'm going to go to her tonight. She needs me. I'm all packed, so I can follow her wherever she wants to go. She's so beautiful.*

If something happens to me, my sister, Jewel Trickney, gets my house, the car, and my rifles. Everything else goes to Bob Valarial.

I'm sure I'll be back to cross this part out later.

It's dark now. I see her at the edge of the woods. She's calling my name. She needs me! <u>She's not the Bloofer Lady.</u>

It was past midnight when Sparkes finished reading this, the journal's last entry. He got up and looked out the window at the same row of trees from which the mysterious Bloofer Lady had appeared. Nothing moved.

Sparkes dressed and went out to the clearing edge, poking around apprehensively with a flashlight. Finding nothing, he gathered his courage and stepped into the line of trees. There his light caught a lump on the ground. Sparkes bent down to examine it.

The remains of a nylon internal frame pack emerged from its retreating cover of snow. Something had ripped it apart. Pieces of clothing and smashed camping gear littered the ground around it. Sparkes saw that whatever slashed the pack went right through it, creating long tears in the back panel and severing some of the binding straps. Dark red-brown stains around the tears on the panel had faded in the rain and snowmelt.

Gingerly, he picked up one loose strap. He read the name "Jerred Trickney" written on the inside of the shoulder pad. Sparkes wondered if bears might have torn it up after Trickney dropped it. He saw plastic food packets all around, gnawed at the corners by voles. Nothing seemed disturbed by anything big enough to inflict that amount of damage to the pack, or to create those stains....

Sparkes passed the remainder of the night in a misery of terror. His loaded rifle lay beside him in the bunk, where he grabbed it at every shift of light or slight sound. At dawn, he calmed enough to carefully check the area for a mile around the cabin. He found no other trace of Trickney, nor did he find any sign of the Bloofer Lady.

Even so, Sparkes fled Butler cabin with a clear sense of being pursued. Immediately upon arriving in Yakutat, he made inquiries. He learned Jerred Trickney had been reported missing in late November. The search for him had eventually been called off. His whereabouts were listed as "unknown."

THE CONSERVER

Doctor Sheldon usually didn't venture into the waiting room. When her nurse told her of the gentleman waiting for her there, he indicated it would be well worth her while to meet the man personally. When she stepped through the security door, past the armed guard, she saw that the nurse was right. She immediately identified the man in the waxed cotton coat, slouch hat, and full beard. A burlap sack hung over one shoulder. Behind his head, she could see a large, black salmon tail.

"Doctor Sheldon?" the man asked, stepping forward and offering a hardened, brown hand. She shook it firmly, and held onto it to guide the man through the security door toward her office.

"Yes, Mister…?"

"Gould," the man replied, "Morgan Gould." She released his hand, as, understanding her intent, he followed her. Neither spoke to the guard who let them pass, a look of naked hunger crossing his face as he saw the man's burden. The doctor led Gould down the hall, carded her office open, and ushered him inside.

"Welcome to Myers Chuck Borough Hospital," the doctor said. The man smiled through his whiskers.

"It's grown some since I last came through," he admitted.

Sheldon laughed, understanding. Ten years ago, no one would have believed that Myers Chuck would grow to its current population, or that it would ever support a hospital. Leveling a steady gaze, Gould came to his point.

"I'd like the new flu cocktails for my wife, two kids, and me. I've brought you this for payment." He had taken the offered seat, and set his bag on the floor. He pulled back the burlap to reveal a perfectly preserved king salmon. Sheldon gasped. "I guess it weighs about 40 pounds," Gould said, quietly.

"My father used to tell stories about king salmon," Sheldon breathed. "How they used to be so plentiful in this part of Alaska."

"The fellows down at the cannery dock cryoed it for me," Gould said. "They say it'll keep perfectly until you're ready to use it." Sheldon's mouth watered uncontrollably at the thought.

"Where did you get it?" she asked, "I've never heard of anyone catching these anymore!"

"Oh," Gould said, his tone and gesture dismissive, rather than evasive, "I come across quite a few out where we live."

"And where is that?" she asked.

"We sail the archipelago," he said. "I caught this particular fish on the far side of Chichagof Island, but I got lucky. We have to go farther out to catch most of them anymore."

"You're a Conserver," Sheldon observed, shifting subjects. The man nodded. "There are coming to be more and more of your kind around here. What's it like? Being a Conserver, I mean."

"It's good," the man said, casting his gaze around her office. "Not like this, of course, but it's what we prefer. We don't need much. What we do need we either get from nature, or we barter for, like this." He touched the salmon with the toe of his boot. Its flash-frozen coating protected it from the dirt, as well as keeping its slime from fouling the tidy carpeting. "Medicine isn't something we need much, but now...."

"Yes, that's interesting—I accept your deal, by the way," she assured him quickly. "But, why do you need flu cocktails? There have been no outbreaks that I've heard of."

"A hunch," Gould admitted. "I'm sure you understand the concerns about exponential population growth."

"You mean the theory that unnaturally sustained populations eventually reach a crisis point, leading to massive die-offs? Of course I've heard of it."

"Well," he smiled, "there you go. The world's gotten so crowded, the crash has to be imminent. They were saying back in the '90s that the next flu epidemic was not a question of when, but how bad? They delayed it some through the last few decades, but I'd say it's coming soon enough to get the cocktails."

"You're probably right," the doctor admitted. "The mixtures we've developed have staved off the worst of it, but the continuing rise of medical costs and increased need is going to allow an epidemic to develop somewhere in the world, even without viral mutations."

"My guess is, it'll start here in Alaska," Gould said, quietly. "We're still caught in the old trap of boom and bust. The current rise in population isn't sustainable. Look at Juneau. They've fought for growth there so aggressively, it was bound to happen. No one would have guessed that area could hold two million people. When I was a boy, they figured it was approaching critical mass at 35,000. Now they've got those anti-grav homes going straight up the mountains on either side of the channel." The doctor nodded gravely. She had toured the so-called "slope slums" on Mount Juneau. Conditions there were ideal for the quick spread of deadly diseases. Even in relatively quiet Myers Chuck, with its mere 50,000 souls, the squalor in certain areas had become shameful.

"When this boom cycles through," the man continued, "it won't be like the last ones. People used to move out of state when times turned poor. This time, there's no place to go. A flu epidemic will be bad, but much less unthinkable than the alternative."

"Which is?"

"Cannibalism. The game's all but gone, for now. The fish stocks are played out. The barnacle industry collapsed three years ago. I figure that was the last of the seafood. There haven't been any affordable food shipments from the lower 48 in seventeen years." Sheldon blushed. People of her class could pay the outrageous prices for imported foodstuffs. "People don't keep pets like they used to. They'll have to eat each other."

"But how can this boom collapse?" Sheldon asked in disbelief. "The water pipeline beats everything that came before—furs, gold, oil, people can learn to live without those things. But not water...."

"True, but water, like everything else, has its limits. They've lowered the quality standards twenty times since the '20s. We're only about two more levels from shipping outright poison. How long will people be willing to buy that, even as bad as the alternatives have become?"

As Gould spoke, Sheldon went to the credenza beside her desk. She began carefully choosing medical items, placing them in a vinyl pouch.

"So, what does one do?" she asked as she worked.

"Head for the hills," Gould chuckled, "or in my case, the ocean. We're almost completely self-sufficient on our sailboat. With the cocktails, and lack of contact, we should just make it." Sheldon turned and gave him a look. "I'm thinking this is our last visit to civilization for at least three years," he told her. "When we set sail from the borough dock, we're mostly on our own until this thing blows over."

Sheldon showed him the cocktails and the applicator, making sure he understood how to use it. She showed him the antibiotics, vitamin supplements, coagulants, beneficial herbs, and other medicines she had included in the pack.

"This is all worth a fortune," Gould protested.

"So's that fish," Sheldon smiled. "We're both getting our money's worth in this deal." She ushered him out of the office and back to the security door.

"You're that certain," Sheldon asked, as he took his leave.

"Dead certain," he smiled. "Best of luck to you, Doc."

"And to you," she said, shaking his hard hand once again.

As he left through the security door, Sheldon caught another, rare glimpse into the hospital waiting room.

So many haggard faces, she mused. Who among them had come to complain of symptoms of the next pandemic?

The Fear

I wasn't even thinking about them when I felt that first tugging bump against my ankle. For once, in this situation, they were the furthest things from my mind. Instead I thought about how good the water felt as I swam, the warmth of the Texas sun, and the attractive young woman who had spread her blanket close to mine on the beach. My mind was blissfully preoccupied when I got hit—not hard, just enough to jerk me downward slightly, making me gulp a mouthful of seawater.

I was confused. I had ventured too far out to hit bottom. No other explanation came to me, until I looked at my foot. I found a raw patch on the outside of my ankle, on the bony knob, a ruddy scrape like a rug burn.

As I stared at the abrasion, I saw movement beneath me. Realization dawned. The water, refreshingly cool before, suddenly seemed icy. I began to shake, my teeth rattling against each other as if about to fall out.

In that instant I felt The Fear.

The Fear developed in me as a child. I think it started after a dream I had in which my older brother and I swam off a low ledge. I sat dangling my feet in the clear water. My brother finished swimming and began to get out. As he boosted himself onto the ledge, I saw two yellow lights deep in the water below. They came toward us so fast they reached the surface just as my brother pulled himself from the water. It was a small shark, about three feet long. Its eyes glowed like light bulbs. It leaped into the air and bit my brother in the back, hitting him with the sound of a baseball bat whacking an inflated inner tube.

I woke up sick and horrified. The images of that dream have never left me. Neither has The Fear.

Sharks fascinated me long before the dream, and my interest only increased afterward. Sharks are cool. They're nature's perfect killing machines, a prehistoric beast virtually unchanged through the eons, with the merciful exception that they seem to have grown smaller. Even though they're found in all oceans, and thousands are caught every day, with hundreds kept for study, they're still largely unknown.

Any kid that spent as much time thinking about sharks as I did would probably feel uneasy stepping into a bathtub, but not me. I loved water. I went swimming whenever I could.

My family lived in Southeast Alaska then, in an island community surrounded by all the water a boy could want. Summers were short and cool, but always offered warmer days when we could grit our teeth and swim in the chilly ocean. Any day that looked promising, I'd usually be the first one in, unless my brother went in before me. Only occasionally would The Fear become unbearable. It would come suddenly, rushing from the back of my mind as I floated in gentle Inside Passage swells with my chin just below the surface. A still, small, perfectly reasonable voice whispered that *sharks could be nearby*. In fact, they could be cruising at that moment between the shore and me. Then came a moment of sickness, hearing—feeling the vibration of that inner tube thud as the dream shark pegged my brother.

It always passed. Common sense, courage, and my love of water pushed The Fear away. Sure, there were sharks, I reasoned. There were also bears in the woods. For that matter, humans surrounded me. I'd known of more people being killed by other people in my town than by sharks.

Sharks really were around. Great whites, the ones we call man-eaters, were supposedly rare in those cold northern waters, but not absent. I thrilled to hear some fishermen had caught a 13-foot great white in their nets. It made news, being fairly unusual, and timely, because the movie, *Jaws* had just been released.

Peter Benchley's film had quite an effect on me. I despised myself for it, but The Fear's small voice grew clearer and more insistent after I watched it. Still, I kept swimming.

Mr. Benchley's book, *The Girl from the Sea of Cortez*, seemed written to correct the misconceptions and sensationalism *Jaws* created. In it he described sharks' attraction to distress vibrations. The book's heroine swam a great distance through the ocean. Sharks ignored her until she began to despair. Then her less-controlled motions attracted their attention. When she calmed down, and began swimming more deliberately again, the sharks lost interest.

Benchley is a noted shark expert, but I later developed an opinion that returned to me as I trod water in the Gulf of Mexico, with a raw and possibly bleeding ankle, and mysterious movement in the water around me. My opinion is, contrary to the claims of many ichthyologists, sharks are truly unpredictable. However much we may know about them, *it is not nearly enough!*

I recalled shark wisdom. "Most shark attacks on humans occur in less than three feet of water." Obviously. If you look for humans in the water, you'll find almost all of them at a depth of less than three feet, so statistically, that's true! This thought afforded me an instant of comic relief before the grimmer possibilities of my situation closed in and The Fear gripped me again.

I had just experienced a "pass" from a shark. It's possible some sharkoid, perhaps an algae sucker without a proper biting mouth, had blundered against me. Possible, but I couldn't take that chance.

Options: Ignore it? It might have been an idle pass, with no real interest. Maybe I communicated the right information: not edible, not worth the effort. Maybe, but I didn't know.

Fight? No knife, I realized, as the Tarzan reflex kicked in, then instantly deflated.

I remembered advice culled from movies: repel a shark with a firm punch to the snout. It might work, if the shark decided to be a sport and attack from the front, in a surface rush from an adequate distance. Besides, having a big brother, I know how futile it is to throw a punch while treading water.

I remembered more advice: soil yourself. Not very elegant, but certainly possible in my present state. I'm sure that would have happened automatically had I anything to offer. Even if I could do any of those things, the big question remained, would they work? I didn't know.

The most sensible option was to slowly, calmly head toward shore. I had ventured farther out than anyone else. I had indulged in a little macho showboating, mostly for the sheer joy of swimming, but also to impress my attractive new friend. I'd pay for it now, apparently.

My mind blanked with a new wave of terror as I felt movement by my leg. Whatever was down there probably measured about four feet, but as it passed close and nudged again, I would have sworn it was much larger. As hideous as the prospect was, I found a slightly consoling element of tragic heroism to being devoured by a large man-eater. More likely, it was a nurse shark, not even a "real" shark, with cruel eyes and triangular fin knifing through the water toward its prey. It didn't matter. It still might kill me. I didn't want to die.

I fought for calm. My teeth still yammered against each other. I vibrated in the water like a badly tuned motor. My body betrayed me, ringing the shark dinner bell. I thought of Benchley and breathed deeply, trying to stop my panic. Slow, deliberate strokes to shore might do it. Slow, deliberate strokes, and I might live. Might...I just didn't know. That was the bottom line: I didn't know. Was it a man-eating shark? Would it lose interest if I could remain calm? *I just didn't know!*

I ducked underwater for an instant, hoping to wash away my fear. A bit calmer, I set my sights on shore, and slowly, carefully, lazily (I hoped) began to swim. I willed myself to breathe evenly. I managed to set a steady pace, even though my scalp crawled and froze with the sensation of being followed. Of that I was dead certain, and nothing in, on, or above the earth could reason with what followed me.

I waited for some sensation, a nibbling at my toes, a scrape along my stomach. I considered crying out, but rejected it. There's a panic vibration a shark could understand! And then, what? Everyone on land freaks out. I'd feed on their fear. I'd be lost for certain. Best to remain calm and keep swimming.

I felt more movement in the water. I submerged, opening my eyes. I saw a dark object below, maybe longer than my body. It cruised toward shore as if it had all the time in the world, which it did. Ancient beast, older than the dinosaurs—if not me, there would be others. But it would certainly have me.

I surfaced and locked my eyes on shore. It didn't seem any closer than a moment ago. My stomach muscles began to contract as if attempting to abandon their position and hide up by my spine. A sickening image filled my head: a sudden locomotive bash against my midriff, and I'm lifted clear of the water by a rush of carnivorous fury. The shoreline shifted crazily. My eyes actually began to roll in my head, I was that deeply into The Fear.

Flashback to a high school professor, who once taught in Australia. He had lovely stories to tell, like an incident that happened to his neighbor. The man went out swimming, got hit by a small shark, got pushed through the water. He escaped with crescent scars from a disinterested bite, and his entire side bruised blue by the force of being pushed through the water by a creature able to exert a biting pressure of *six thousand pounds per square half-inch!* There's a thought to keep me warm at night. Or freeze my blood in the gulf coast summer sun. I tried to swim faster.

Was my ankle bleeding, putting out a blood trail? That's one everybody knows. After all, what's chum for? I wanted to assume the fetal position, give up, make myself a big meat pill. Take me in one swallow. You got me, I won't fight. Just don't tear me apart—don't hurt me. To me, death isn't so frightening as the possibility of excruciating pain. And few things ever hurt me like being scared. Really scared.

I stalled, my mind wandering, my body unable to do its job without guidance. I wondered if I was going into shock. Would I know if I were? I took deep breaths, focused on shore again, and swam. I stroked in time to the steady beat in my head and chest. It sounded exactly like a baseball bat whacking an inflated inner tube.

My throat burned from the salt water I'd swallowed. My shoulders hurt. It's good for me, I thought. Right. "Coroners were unable to identify the body, but they did say the man was in pretty good shape." I began to giggle crazily, but stifled it. What kind of vibration would *that* set off? I didn't know.

The beach seemed a little closer. Instead of focusing on the movement in the water around me, I scanned the shore. No one was standing, pointing, or yelling. My new friend watched me mildly. Or maybe her eyes were closed. Was a knifepoint fin slicing through my wake?

The water near me boiled with activity. I waited for a sudden jerk. I held each breath, ready to be dragged under without warning. Something definitely moved just behind my kicking feet. My soles pricked as if about to be tickled. Stay calm, pray for shore, and swim...swim....

◆ ◆ ◆ ◆ ◆

It's a cold night. I sit by my window, gazing out over Sitka Sound. I wonder if sharks cruise these waters tonight, as I remember that summer day in the Gulf of Mexico.

I was confused when I realized I wasn't dead. The newspaper reported I had been attacked in three feet of water, then saved by onlookers. Experts judged it to be a young blue shark, possibly six feet long, but they weren't sure. I certainly don't know. Now that it's all over, I no longer care. I know I'm alive. That's good enough.

The irony of the situation never occurred to me until much later. How many people, I wonder, live their whole lives in fear of an event that is so unlikely that it never happens to them? How is it that the thing I feared happened to me? Did fearing it make it my reality? Is my life more fulfilled in some strange way, than those people whose fears never materialize?

I think about that on nights like this especially, when cold weather makes my leg ache. I'm very lucky the shark only took it just above the knee.

I shift to a more comfortable position in my easy chair and continue to gaze at the sound, pulling my blanket tighter around my shoulders to ward off the cold, and to ward off The Fear.

THE CRY OF A LOON

Wallace Norton waited five years to hear the cry of a loon. He had no idea that on the evening he finally heard it, he would have only moments in which to savor it.

Wallace loved loons long before they became a trendy decoration on coffee mugs and Christmas trees. His affection developed one afternoon as he sat in his aunt's parlor. His aunt was playing a scratchy nature record. Wallace paged through a picture book, trying to ignore the cacophony of woodland birdcalls ricocheting through the room. He turned a page to discover a photo of a darkly wooded island, shrouded in mist, surrounded by mirror-surfaced water, just as a sound leapt from the old hi-fi speakers into his soul.

How does one describe a loon's cry? It's a ululation, a cackle, a sigh. It's a mournful ghost trying unsuccessfully to whistle a happy tune. Accompanied by classical or slick new-age music, it can be soothing, comforting. Heard in the wild, with dark coming on fast, strange shapes shifting in the bush, and you miles from home, it can be as calming as a death-knell.

Wallace sat transfixed by the photo of the fog bound island—Shaman Island, near Juneau, Alaska, the caption read—and the cry of a loon.

The next morning Wallace left for Alaska.

For the next five years Wallace worked and played in his adopted state. He had always lived an outdoorsman's lifestyle, and adapted well. His outdoor activities should have provided ample opportunity to hear loons. He saw many of them on remote lakes or drifting off the rocky shores in tidewater. Never, in all that time, did he hear one call. Never, until the evening he disappeared.

Wallace collected loon recordings. He listened to them on quiet evenings, his work done and the fire low. He never ceased to thrill to the chuckle, the wail, the song. He learned that a local Tlingit clan had adopted the loon as their crest, because their ancestors, lost in darkness or fog, once followed a loon's call to safety. As much as he loved the sound, Wallace felt if he were lost, the loon's eerie cry would be the last sound he'd want to follow anywhere.

His perpetual hope to hear a loon in the wild made Wallace pause that chilly afternoon, the rain pouring down around him, surrendering to the sensation of being engulfed.

Perhaps you've felt it? It comes when the air feels just so, when, as it often does in Southeast Alaska, the sky lowers until it sits on your shoulders. Rain falls in a steady white-noise hiss, dulling your senses, numbing your mind. It's then, usually as you stand on a gravel beach, looking at the forest starting thick and menacing at the top of the scrim, a shiver hits you. Then your less rational side wonders who or what is staring at you from that forest, wanting you dead.

Wallace pulled his kayak above the tide line, securing it to a stump half-buried on the beach. He unlimbered his rifle against the possibility of bears, though his wilder side whispered of other danger. He felt confused by his sudden urge to be home, his shutters closed against the forest night. He hesitated, staring hard to pierce the black tree line through falling rain and gathering darkness. No sight or sound to suggest, but something moved in the moss-hung trees and devil's club tangles. Something big.

Laughter split the silence, rattling the beach, echoing through groves of spruce and hemlock. A pair of ravens, giant, black, crested, with scraggy neck feathers, spooked from their treetop hideout. Their sweeping wings cut the air with swishing whistles as they cruised by, croaking deep admonishments as they passed. Wallace laughed away his shame at standing weak-kneed in the cold, fearing the unknown. He was in his element. *He* was the unseen creature that moved through the forest, and a warm campsite awaited him there. It was time for action, not woolgathering or cowering. He shouldered his gear and climbed the beach.

At forest's edge he stopped, ears straining. Across the rain-pocked inlet he heard a high, wavering cry.

He heard it again.

The cry of a loon came from somewhere on the water, shrouded by mist and rain splash.

Wallace scanned the inlet. Vaguely, he made out white specks on black feathers contrasting with gray-green water, as a single loon floated into view. He watched, entranced, as it lifted its head and uttered its lonely, mournful, beautiful cry once more.

At that precise moment, something pulled Wallace abruptly backward so quickly the forest seemed, in an instant, to swallow him. The loon, suddenly alone, bobbed peacefully, undisturbed and unaware on the glassy water.

Searchers found Wallace Norton's rifle rusting where it had fallen. They discovered his kayak floating free, miles from the spot. The man himself was not seen again.

GHOST WANTED

Alan flipped through television channels on his day off. His friends worked on different schedules, so he had no one to hang around with. He had finished reading a novel two hours before. His did his household chores the previous evening to keep his day off free.

He risked becoming very bored.

At that time of day, the T.V. schedule offered game shows and soap operas, but Alan subscribed to cable. He flipped toward the movie channels, half hoping to find an "R" rated feature, full of sex and creatively executed mayhem.

He paused at one channel when he recognized the Terrytoons theme, announcing the beginning of a cartoon. From the style of the opening graphics, Alan guessed this one dated from the late 1950s. He stared at the screen, idly scratching in impolite places as the action began.

A cute, juvenile ghost, possibly a prototype Casper or Spooky, appeared on screen. The tyke read a newspaper want ad. The ad's text appeared long enough for most viewers to read it, but in Alan's lethargic mood he barely caught it. It requested a ghost to haunt a house.

Alan sat up abruptly. What a great idea! He snapped the television off, not bothering to learn what happened to the little ghost. He had found something to do at last.

Alan loved subtle practical jokes. He specialized in pranks so obscure they went unnoticed by all but a very few particularly observant people. He fancied himself a master of understatement, perpetrating stunts within full view of thousands of people, yet going undetected by all but one or two.

While vacationing in Seattle, he visited the Space Needle. At the top of the towering landmark he leaned out past the guardrail. Using a pair of toy boots on his first two fingers, he made a little path of footprints leading straight off the ledge. He knew the prints wouldn't last long in Seattle's rainy climate. They would probably wash away before anyone noticed, but that didn't matter. His satisfaction came from knowing he had done it, knowing someone might see, and wonder.

One year, Alan's college theater department staged *A Midsummer Night's Dream*. The lighting crew designed a delightful sunset and moonrise. One night Alan added his own touch to the rising moon: the faint silhouette of a witch riding a broomstick. An accomplice urged him to do it again the next night, but for Alan the beauty of the trick lay in doing it only once. Very few people noticed the witch, but those who did talked of it for years afterward.

Alan's coworkers learned to be very wary, always waiting for the next joke. Alan did very little at all, enjoying the daily search for his handiwork. Most of the stunts they "uncovered" proved to be the product of their own paranoia rather than Alan's mind. He *had* been the one who scattered pieces of a toy skeleton under the copy machine. He waited four years for the machine to get moved. The discovery created a small commotion. Paranoia levels increased dramatically for a time.

Six months had passed since Alan's last prank. "It's time," he told himself as he sat down at his typewriter and composed a letter to the Want Ad Editor of his local newspaper, containing the following:

WANTED TO HAUNT:
A ghost to occupy and terrify 2247 East Pasqual Road. Must be experienced. Females encouraged. Apply in person.

Alan closed the letter appropriately and wrote a check to cover the cost. He smiled as he addressed and stamped the envelope. He chuckled as he stepped out to the corner drop box.

Walking back up the hill, Alan surveyed his property. He had been raised in this fine old two-story Victorian. He had always thought it would make a perfect haunted house. Anyone who read his ad and decided to check the address would be pleased. This house obviously needed a ghost. That made the whole idea sweeter.

Three days later, Alan checked the evening paper and found his ad. Carefully, he clipped it and took it to his file cabinet. He kept a folder of newspaper articles and other souvenirs of his pranks. It wasn't very full, since most of his activities went unnoticed by the press. Alan hoped to keep the file as empty as possible, regarding media attention as more failure than success. He considered the file more precious to him than the insurance policies and other important papers he kept in the cabinet.

The door chime rang just as Alan replaced the folder and locked the drawer. He walked to the foyer in high spirits. Here was a new challenge: entertaining friends while in his fresh excitement. As a rule he never discussed his pranks, and he felt particularly tempted to share this one.

The front door swung open on an empty porch. No one appeared to be there. Alan snorted and began to close the door. Ringing the doorbell and running away was not his idea of high art in the prankster world.

The door almost shut before he heard a small, polite sound, like a clearing throat. Curious, Alan opened the door again.

The hot day's warmth lingered into evening, but Alan felt a cold draft encircle him. In the porch lamp's glow he could barely make out a shimmering, milky light. It reminded Alan of the aurora borealis, which he had seen once when his family had traveled to Canada. Now, standing in his doorway, it seemed as if that electromagnetic phenomenon had somehow manifested itself on his front porch. Again he heard the throaty noise. The light congealed into a vaguely human form.

"Good evening," intoned a voice. It sounded deep yet reedy, with a transparent quality like low notes on a glass flute.

Alan stepped back, startled.

"Good evening," the voice repeated. "My name is Arthur Gwaingellen. I've come to apply for your haunting position."

At these words the figure solidified further, its features becoming clearer. Alan perceived a human skull draped with a large silk cloth. He saw the definite outline of a cranial bone at the top of the figure. Two eye sockets appeared in appropriate position. Somewhere within each socket a mellow light glowed brighter than the surrounding mist. Below the eyes gaped the manic, toothy grimace of a naked skull, but undulating white light played across it to somehow suggest a polite smile—anticipatory, even businesslike. Alan saw the outlines of shoulders and torso, but beyond that the figure faded in and out of visibility, wavering like smoke in a breeze.

Alan observed this in less than a second. He came to a quick conclusion: some clever person, some wily kindred spirit, had answered his ad. This must be an extremely sophisticated projection, perhaps even a hologram. He knew what to do. He stepped back, grinning widely.

"Of course!" he practically shouted. "Yes, of course. Please, come inside!" He held the door open, making a sweeping gesture of welcome. He knew what had to happen next. The projection, if its operator could manipulate it to do so, must decline. To enter the house would mean moving the projector, possibly into Alan's line of sight. Very likely the projection wouldn't work at all inside his well-lit parlor. Closing the door would certainly interrupt the projection beams, making the apparition disappear. The joke's perpetrator would have to refuse or risk exposure.

Nothing of the sort happened. The specter inclined its head graciously and passed easily through the doorway. Alan swung the door shut, stubbornly pursuing his hypothesis, even as the figure glided down the hallway.

The door closed, but the visitor did not disappear.

Surprised, Alan immediately rethought his position. This could not be a projection. If a product of technology, it was advanced far beyond anything he had known. It couldn't be, but it might be...*must* be—a ghost! As incredible as that seemed, no other explanation short of dreaming or hallucination approached logic, based on the evidence at hand.

Recovering quickly, Alan led his strange guest into the parlor, where, after only the slightest hesitation, during which Ebenezer Scrooge flashed through his mind, he offered a seat. He watched closely, wondering if the wraith would clear its flowing shroud like a skirt before seating itself.

It didn't. That which had been Arthur Gwaingellen simply sank down to the offered chair gracefully and silently. Alan hurried to his own seat.

Alan found himself in a totally unexpected situation, but he thought it best to keep whatever advantage he could find.

"Now then, Mister, ah...Gwaingellen," he began, "you are interested in the position I advertised in the paper. May I know your qualifications?"

Hands emerged on either side of the apparition, met at lap level, and clasped.

"I have been in this state of being for several centuries," the ghost told him. "I was a minor Scottish lord, foully murdered by my brothers during a hunting trip. I believe you know that betrayed and murdered men of stature make the very best haunts." Again the milky white light, ("His *ectoplasm*," Alan thought) created the appearance of a smile. Alan recognized the expression of one who is reluctant to boast of personal accomplishments, but realizes the need to mention them.

"I spent my early years in the finest castles and estates of my homeland," the spirit continued. "I'm also proud to say I spent considerable time in Eastern Europe, in the Carpathian Mountains."

"You mean..." asked Alan, forgetting his unease.

"Yes," Arthur assured him, "Transylvania. Fascinating place. Highly superstitious people. I took great pleasure haunting there, despite rather enthusiastic competition from...locals."

"How did you arrive in America?"

"I had been haunting an elderly couple in a lovely cottage outside Portsmouth, England," the specter replied, again with a suggestion of a pleasant smile over the garish grin of skeletal jaws. "One of their children, an adventurous lad, came to bid them farewell before journeying to the United States. He anticipated so many exciting new opportunities there, I decided to accompany him. My efforts had quite worn out the poor old couple by then. I really had grown quite fond of them. I felt it best to leave them in peace."

"How kind," Alan mused. He struggled to regain his businesslike demeanor. "How did you come to leave your last position?" he asked.

Arthur chuckled hollowly. "Urban renewal, no more, no less. I occupied a sturdy little Cape Cod in the next city over for several years. No one lived there, but children came from miles around to test their bravery, and my skill." The ghost waxed nostalgic as he spoke. "Halloween was the very best, of course, but I kept very busy always—very busy indeed. That is, until bulldozers came, and construction began." He sighed. "Tract housing is so...*unghostly*, don't you think?" Alan found himself nodding in agreement.

"Then I saw your ad," the spirit continued, "which I found delightful. Like so many, my profession is not the kind that finds openings listed in newspapers. Still, when one needs work, one checks all sources."

Alan realized his predicament. The ad had been a joke, after all, not intended to get a serious response. He had let it go this far through sheer astonishment. It looked as if he might have to see it through, like it or not.

"What sort of payment would you expect to haunt this house?" he asked. He did well at his job, but perhaps not well enough to support a career spook.

"Room would be sufficient," said Arthur. "I need only a place to be."

"And board?" asked Alan.

"Room." The ghost repeated the word politely but firmly. "That is all. You see, by gaining your permission to haunt, I provide myself a form of security that is hard to come by in the spirit world."

Alan felt slightly relieved. The price was right, but he still didn't want or need a ghost, despite earlier thoughts on the matter. He liked his house well enough without a haunt, thank you.

"Naturally, in return for a place, I would have to satisfy *your* needs," Arthur continued. "I believe the word used in the ad was 'terrify.'"

"Yes," agreed Alan, suddenly seeing a way out. "That's important!"

"Well, then," said Arthur, as he levitated from the chair, "Perhaps it's time to...audition."

With that, the spirit became a blurred streak of pale light that elongated toward the ceiling until it disappeared through it with an audible *swoosh*.

Alan sat alone in his parlor for a moment, wondering what, if anything, had actually just happened. Could it all have been his imagination? After a moment's thought he picked up the phone beside him and dialed his best friend's number.

"Carl, this is Alan—"

"Hi, buddy, what's up?"

"If I told you, you wouldn't believe me," Alan laughed. "Can you come over right now? I have something I'd really like you to see."

"No problem," his friend replied. "I've just got one or two things to finish up here, then I'll be over."

"Great, Carl. Thanks."

As he set the receiver down, he felt the hair on the back of his neck begin to tingle. The parlor had been well lit a moment ago, but the lamps had dimmed without Alan's noticing. His feeling of unease increased. He felt cold.

He recognized the same chill he had felt in Arthur's presence. He relaxed, realizing the ghost had returned from wherever he'd gone. He wasn't bothered by the sound of heavy dragging footsteps behind him. His pulse didn't quicken with anticipation when the footfalls stopped abruptly. He felt no anxiety waiting for them to continue. He jumped, but only slightly, when an icy, skeletal hand touched his shoulder. He relaxed again as it began to move up the side of his neck and caress his cheek with a feathery touch. He became slightly surprised when the hand pulled his head back and he felt a straight razor placed next to his carotid artery. When he felt the razor slash his throat from the base of one ear to the other in a quick, clean motion he became decidedly curious. Finally, he could no longer resist the urge to gently finger his throat, which he found to be perfectly intact.

"My word," came Arthur's voice behind him. "I really must congratulate you. You have quite a fine nerve, especially for one so young. That little trick has killed stouter men than you from sheer fright." The ghost faded into visibility as he floated around to face Alan. "Still," continued Arthur, "if I want this job, I *must* terrify you one way or another."

The spirit raised his arms above his head. Instantly he changed from a shrouded wraith to a full human skeleton. This brought no real response from Alan, save for an expression of keen interest. The clean white bones began to change, darkening as if from exposure to bad weather. Bits of putrefying flesh and dead vegetation sprouted everywhere. Empty eye sockets filled with staring eyeballs, one directed at Alan, the other rolling to the left. Still Alan didn't respond. The skeleton began to writhe and shake as if in great pain. The jaw dropped open and began to scream.

Alan winced slightly as the noise seemed to pierce his eardrums, but he quickly adjusted to the volume. The flesh of the skeleton began to freshen and rejuvenate, particularly on one side of the skull, until Alan could clearly see that the face was his own mother's. The voice became hers as well, howling in unknown agony. Alan kept his composure, although he paled, and his eyes widened.

"That's getting there," his mother cried, "but it's not quite terror!"

At the word "terror," his mother's face became whole for an instant before bursting into flames. The fire reached the ceiling immediately, but didn't burn any part of it. Dark, oily smoke rolled out in all directions, then vanished. The smell of burning flesh and hair became overpowering. Alan's mother's face dripped, ran, and bubbled away.

The effect was the most gruesome sight Alan had beheld in his life, but it came too late.

Arthur Gwaingellen's quick check on the progress of his fear had struck Alan as extremely funny. He laughed so hard he choked and sputtered. His mother and her conflagration disappeared at once. Arthur returned to his billowy, translucent state. He seemed quite deflated.

"You, Sir, are a very brave man." The ghost collapsed in the chair he had occupied before.

"I'm sorry," giggled Alan, struggling to control himself. "I guess ghostly stuff just doesn't terrify me that much. You almost had me when you were doing my mom. That was really something!"

"Yes, something," murmured the ghost. "But it obviously wasn't enough. You advertised for a ghost to terrify this house. I've not done that yet."

"Look, Arthur, it's really okay," laughed Alan, waving his hand. "You don't quite understand my reasons—"

"But you see," Arthur interrupted, rising from the chair. "Everyone is terrified by something. The key to this puzzle is finding out what frightens you in particular."

"But you don't understand—" Alan tried again. The specter raised a hand to stop him.

"Silence!" he cried, "I must think."

He glided back and forth in an unintentional parody of pacing. Alan gave up trying to explain. He sat back in his chair, watching the wraith. In all the excitement, he hadn't quite grasped the fact he was spending the evening with a resident of the spirit world—certainly not his usual Thursday evening activity.

The ghost crossed back and forth in silence for a moment or two. Finally he stopped, turning to Alan with an air of triumph.

"I've got it!" he announced. He darted over to the wall behind Alan's chair, to a stereo system there. He scanned Alan's rack of compact discs for a moment, selected one and came back around to face Alan.

"This is most interesting," he said, studying the CD in his hand. "A copy of *Lady Destiny* by the Purben Seven. Most interesting indeed."

Alan had grown noticeably uncomfortable.

"I see it's autographed by the entire band," the ghost continued. "It must be extremely valuable since only 4,000 copies were printed before they stopped production after the entire group died in that accident." He removed the disc from its jewel box and studied it. "I hear these devices are nearly indestructible. I wonder...."

He turned and approached the nearest floor lamp. As he drew near, its bulb brightened far beyond its 100 watts. Alan could feel the heat of it from his seat across the room. With an air of great curiosity, the spirit held the disc over the light, lowering it slowly toward the superheated bulb.

"Don't do that!" Alan yelled. He leapt up and dove across the room. As his fingers closed around the CD, the ghost disappeared. The disc snaked out of Alan's grasp. It whirled to the next lamp and hovered, as its bulb grew abnormally bright. The disc began to discolor as Alan moaned in disbelief. He lunged again. The disc whisked past him back to the first light where it continued to deteriorate. The ghost rematerialized, dropping the CD.

"This is quite unpleasant, and highly unsporting," he complained. "Unfortunately, one doesn't find many positions for haunts these days. I find it necessary to use whatever means possible to terrify."

"But this is vandalism!" sputtered Alan. "It's hoodlumism, not fright!"

"Do you mean to say the loss of valuable possessions doesn't terrify you?" Arthur asked as he faded from view. On the fireplace mantle an antique vase began to totter.

"Not *that!*" screamed Alan, "It's worth a fortune!"

Again he dove across the room, arriving too late to catch the vase as it tipped onto the floor and shattered. Arthur reappeared long enough to show that he moved toward the dining room before vanishing again. It took Alan a second to realize where the ghost had gone: to an antique hutch filled with his family's crystal. The entire collection had survived six generations. Not one piece was chipped.

"Until now," Alan moaned, then sobbed as he heard the hutch fall forward with a deafening crash. The air flickered in front of his face as the wraith passed through on his way to other mischief.

"I have always considered poltergeists the lowest form of haunting," Arthur's voice came to him out of the air close to his left ear. "It lacks the discipline called for in this line of work. Now that I've tried it, however, I find a certain attraction to the violence of it." The voice faded away toward the stairs. A line of framed photographs on the wall fell to the floor.

The situation had gotten completely out of hand. Alan had to get rid of Arthur—but how? Tell him the audition was over? "Thank you for your time, leave your resume with my secretary, we'll make our decision sometime next week?" The ghost seemed determined to get the job at all costs. Alan ruled out exorcism almost immediately. Finding and soliciting the help of a priest would take more time than he appeared to have.

"Besides," he mused, "I'm not Catholic!"

He began to cast about his memory for folk remedies he had learned through years of reading. He knew all about how one is supposed to lay a vampire. Those traditions crowded his memory, making his task more difficult. He tried to remember the "real" ghost stories he'd read so avidly as a boy.

He heard pandemonium above his head. Arthur had apparently found his bedroom, and his mother's collection of china from occupied Japan.

A thought occurred to him. Had he read something about hospitality? Didn't some people believe offering a spirit food would appease it?

He had read too much fiction. Fiction writers are noted for their willingness to choose a supernatural character's boundaries, ignoring any "traditional" limitations that didn't fit the plot. A certain writer of vampire fiction once went to great lengths to claim vampires are immune to crucifixes, but maintained a vampire can only enter a dwelling with the householder's permission, simply to build momentary suspense in a minor scene. Alan sorted through devices of this kind in his search for a solution to his problem. To complicate matters, a credible person must assume all one reads about the supernatural is actually fiction. If Alan accepted that, he had to acknowledge that any method he chose might not work at all!

Still, a solution must be found soon, Alan decided, as the sound of destruction increased upstairs.

He forced himself to focus on food. Some Eastern ancestor worship traditions involved feeding spirits, didn't they? The phrase "unquiet dead" popped into his mind. Wasn't that the idea: spirits haunt because they're restless, uncomfortable? This might be the answer. Part of making a guest comfortable includes offering food. It seemed the best he could do. It was worth trying.

Alan ran into the kitchen, wishing Carl would hurry up and arrive. Maybe he had a better idea for getting rid of Arthur.

He wondered what a ghost would eat. More to the point, what *could* a ghost eat?

As he searched, he remembered something from earlier in the evening. When he had discussed pay with Arthur, he had asked if board should be included. The ghost had rather emphatically stated he only needed room. Maybe he was on the right track. He worked faster, encouraged by this new hope, and the continuing noise from upstairs. He selected several types of cheese, an apple, and a pear. He sliced them neatly and arranged them on a serving plate. He didn't know if presentation counted, but hospitality might be a key factor. He carried the plate and a glass of wine into the parlor, where he placed them on a coffee table.

Alan sat in his chair and tried to relax. Since Arthur was still auditioning, he assumed he would check on the progress of Alan's fear shortly.

Arthur appeared seconds later. He drifted through the room with an armload of papers. Alan paled as he recognized his prank clippings folder among other important documents. As Arthur approached the fireplace, logs stacked there began to crackle. Flames popped up, burning cheerily.

"Mr. Gwaingellen," Alan called, trying hard not to shout in his urgency. "I'm—really quite impressed by your performance. You must be tired from all your haunting."

"Tut, Sir," the ghost smiled, "I take great pride in my work. You have obviously not reached an appropriate level of fear. I still have much to do!"

"All the more reason to take a break," Alan croaked, a bit hastily. He struggled to keep a cordial tone despite his rising panic. "Look, I've prepared a snack for you. Please forgive my negligence. I should have offered you something to begin with."

The spirit paused, Alan's prank file poised above the flames. He seemed indecisive.

"Why...thank you," he stammered. "You are most kind." He set the papers down on the floor before the fireplace, and stepped tentatively toward the food. With a gracious nod toward Alan, he lifted the glass of wine and a piece of cheese.

The ghost began to nibble. He seated himself and ate. Alan watched eagerly. The ghost *could* eat, that much was clear. He was amazed the translucent entity could consume solid food. The question remained whether or not food would make the ghost leave. Assuming it did, what exactly would happen? Would he fade away, or explode, or would he excuse himself and depart through the front door?

The spirit of Arthur Gwaingellen did none of that. He calmly ate his fill, then leaned back in his chair, sighed, and, as a slightly distressed expression played across his face, vanished with a small popping sound.

Alan felt slightly disappointed. As minutes passed, and the ghost failed to reappear, Alan became almost frantic with curiosity. Half an hour later, the ghost had not returned. Alan decided it truly must be gone.

Had it left because Alan had fed it, or for some other reason? He began to wish Arthur would return so he could question him, but his eye fell on the papers by the fire, and the remains of the shattered vase. Leaping to his feet, he gathered the papers and returned them to his file cabinet.

"What a night," he commented aloud. "I wish Carl would show up. I can't wait to tell him about it!"

As if in answer, the front door chime rang. Alan locked the file drawer and ran to the door. Getting Carl to believe any of what had just happened would be a challenge. He felt up to it, though. With a broad grin, he pulled the door open wide.

A chill fell on him instantly. Before him floated the figure of a beautiful young woman, flickering and translucent, like the aurora borealis.

Hello," the specter said in a voice like wind through reeds on a riverbank. "I've come to apply for the haunting position you advertised in the newspaper."

LONG BLACK VEIL

On nights like this, when storms rage in from the ocean, she visits her lover.

When the glass drops and the hour grows late, she steals from her marriage bed, bundles herself in her dark woolen cloak, secrets her identity in a long black veil, and walks the harbor road to the cemetery. There she finds the place they laid her lover to rest.

Unseen, she settles, resting against the massive stone. She mourns his passing in silence, longing for the feel of his body next to hers, the warmth of his breath in her hair, the sweetness of stolen hours.

On many of these visits she watches, with an amazing detachment, other activities in the graveyard.

Creatures beyond imagining come down from the forested mountains, into the cemetery. They take advantage of the same covering storms that allow her to visit her lover's grave. The howling wind and the hiss of driving rain mask from human ears the wild laughter, cries and scrabbling of a hideous mob of beings.

Vaguely human in shape and deportment, they differ as markedly from mankind as they do from each other. She has roused herself from her mourning to observe them closely. Some have long beaks and black, shining eyes, like monstrous cousins of the ravens that haunt the region. Others sport fangs of startling length and sharpness, shining from wide, flat, noseless faces. Some are hirsute, others obscenely naked, fishy white in the light of the riding moon that peeps from scudding clouds. Some individuals she can never quite see, her whole attention being arrested by their large eyes that seem windows of pure evil. Others, she believes, have no eyes at all, or squint like moles. They seem dressed, such as they are, in moldering casts-offs, mixtures of clothing styles and eras as astonishing as the variety in their physical appearance.

Their errand among the dead is hideous. Descending upon this or that grave, they attack the earth, upending headstones, cracking crypts, digging with their claws until the soil is piled high all around. Once they have unearthed their victim, they give themselves over to orgiastic feasting. Snapping with tooth and beak, they tear the remains of the dead asunder, devouring the decaying flesh and bones.

They are ghouls, feeding on the unfortunate dead.

So great is her love for the man she mourns that these activities cannot drive her away. For their part, the creatures seem to have but one singular mission among humans. She has watched them on many nights, allowing them to pass quite near her, but they never molest her. She feels very little fear of them, or of anything. She carries, in the folds of her voluminous cloak, her lover's Winchester rifle. She used this same weapon the previous spring, when a brown bear interrupted an afternoon's lovemaking in her lover's cabin on Gold Creek.

She delighted to break away from her lover's embrace when their activity reached a certain heat. She would rush outside and bathe in the snow, then return taut and tingling to bed. The bear, drawn to the food cache near the cabin, surprised her as she stepped out the front door, stripped to the waist and glowing. It reared and lunged, while she calmly reached through the doorway for the rifle. She cocked it, swung it to her bare shoulder and fired in the breadth of an instant, dropping the beast at her feet with a single round. Afterward, the lovers often frolicked on the cabin floor, wrapped in the bear's capacious pelt. The image of her, brazenly naked above her long skirt, high-piled hair haloed in fly-aways from their amorous tussling, drawing a quick bead on the huge creature, stayed with her lover forever after.

Ownership of that particular rifle could encourage uncomfortable questions. It is hard to guess where she keeps it in her house, away from chance discovery by her husband.

Incredibly, the ghouls' strange activities go undetected by the townspeople. Their revelry uproots and destroys graves. Yet, once their vile appetites are sated, the beasts somehow manage to return the scene of their crime to a state so closely resembling its original that none would know the dead have been so disturbed.

And what of that, she must wonder? After one dies, what does the disposal of the body really matter? Do the dead care? She thinks not.

She does become curious, eventually. She notes that these strange beings go directly to specific graves in the cemetery. They commit their desecrations against a single resident each night. She begins to wait until the ghouls have set things to right and raced cackling and screeching back into the mountains. She then draws near the defiled grave to learn the victim's identity.

She begins to see a pattern.

Once she has sensed a common link among the victims, she begins to take more careful notice of the ghoulish activities. She also sets her mind to remembering which graves had been visited before she took such particular interest. Many of the names she knows, for she and her husband lived in the town long before the gold rush swelled its population. Sometimes this victim or another seems so unlikely, she feels her theory proved false. However, as the pattern continues until she can almost predict the ghouls' choices beforehand, she reassesses her opinion of the more implausible victims. It even gives her some wicked pleasure to speculate on the possible conspirators of the disturbed dead.

She also begins to give more thought to how these attacks might matter to the deceased. This concern is heightened both by the observation of the pattern, and the perception of something else.

She notices one of the many unpleasant and unattributable sounds heard during each attack on a grave is a high, thin scream, much like a strong wind forcing its way through a chink in a cabin wall. Eventually, she discovers this alarming sound is never heard during the unearthing of the casket—it begins with the first terrible grasping and rending of the corpse itself. With growing unease, she realizes it does not die away until the grisly business is complete.

Melancholy seizes her mind, and no little dread, to imagine this sound the cries of a soul being torn, flayed and devoured by the creature's cruel beaks, fangs and claws.

Once her belief in the common link among the ghouls' victims is firm, she resolves to be ever more faithful in her visits to her lover's grave. She takes greater risks, going out more often, and on less inclement nights than she had used. Her time in the cemetery becomes less one of mourning than of watchfulness. The Winchester rifle, which before had stayed secreted in the folds of her dark cloak, now warms against her thigh. Her long, delicate fingers curl around the stock, close to the trigger. She stays longer than she has ever dared before, if the creatures are slow in coming. Many times she stumbles home, exhausted, shortly before her husband wakes in the morning. She begins to fear for her health.

Ironically, her husband is the one to take sick.

His illness drags on for many weeks, causing him great discomfort. He sleeps fitfully, so that through the whole time she dares not slip away to the cemetery. She dutifully nurses the man as well as she can. Her thoughts, however, are always down the road, especially on nights when the glass falls and fierce storms roll in from the cold north Pacific. She can't summon pretext to visit the cemetery during the day to check for the subtle signs of disturbance that only she would recognize. Her husband's convalescence comes slowly. Anxiety torments her until she can return to her nocturnal habit.

Finally, the husband recovers enough to sleep soundly through the night once again. The very next evening a gale kicks up, and she wraps herself in her wool cloak, not forgetting the rifle, hides her face in her long black veil, and hurries to the cemetery.

She has not been seated long on the great stone of her lover's grave, when, carried on the storm winds, she hears the sounds of the ghouls' approach. Their shrieks and inhuman laughter, their barks and shouts unnerve her slightly, but she who faced the charging brown bear will not be daunted even by this horrid mob. They fly down the mountain and into the cemetery, making their raucous way toward the very spot on which she sits. When she realizes their goal, she raises the rifle and cranks the lever, chambering a round.

The creatures shamble close until, suddenly aware of her, they stop. She stands to face them, the rifle held muzzle down in front of her, ready to rise to her shoulder on the instant. She almost shouts a warning, but realizes she has never, in all the times she has observed them, heard a word pass among them, and so keeps silent. She steels herself as they examine her with their baleful eyes. Their stench overpowers her—the corruption of the grave is on their breath. Their clothing reeks of mold and offal. Their fantastic, unnatural forms chill her, but she stands firm. One of them, with large jagged teeth and the dead eyes of a shark, takes a step toward her. She brings the rifle to her shoulder and waits.

The beasts burst into raucous laughter, gibbering, baying. They advance on her as one, and before she can fire her weapon, they roughly push her aside. She falls against a nearby headstone, dazed, tangled in her cloak. Taking no further notice of her, the ghouls set about unearthing the body of her dead lover. She finds her feet, pulling herself up on the headstone and grasping it for support. She stares, unable to look away from the excavation taking place in front of her.

The pattern she suspected is confirmed. It is clear from her expression she realizes, unmistakably, that a similar fate awaits her upon her own death. These creatures will visit her as they visited each person in the cemetery who had indulged in adultery during life. And, as the fiends unearth and breach the casket lid, as long, powerfully muscled arms reach in and withdraw their prey, the keening begins. She screams, staggering away, understanding the truth: the soul, hovering near its mortal remains, can and does feel the horror, the agony of being consumed by these ghouls.

I had hoped to spare her this last, awful knowledge, but as the claws, beaks and terrible teeth of my tormentors close upon my dead flesh, pain and fear rise within me as a shriek so loud it overcomes even the silence of my grave. At last, my dead voice carries a message to my love—not of comfort or desire, as I had so often wished—but of abysmal despair.

WHISPERS IN THE TREES

I will not go with you to the edge of the forest. I won't follow you into the trees. You're new here. You didn't grow up, like I did, listening for the whispers in the trees. I know better. I'll stay right here and wait to see if you come back out.

You paid me to come here, so you must know some of the story. My sister, Breanne, and I grew up in Juneau. Our parents raised us to understand this country, to look for the opportunities and dangers in the change of the tide, the shifts in the weather, the moods of the rainforest and its inhabitants. They taught us what they could, but they didn't know about everything here that should be feared.

One afternoon, when I was pretty young, Breanne and I pulled our kayaks up on this beach. I remember the look on her face as we stood in the rain. I didn't spook easily in those days, but something made me cautious that time. I strained to hear above the drumming of the rain. I thought I heard a sighing noise among the trees at the forest edge, a sound of wind where none blew.

I looked sidelong at Breanne, who appeared to hear it, too. She turned and popped the binders holding her rifle in its waterproof case. She carried the weapon on these trips to make Dad happy, but as a point of honor she never used it, or even removed it from the case, as she did now. She pushed cartridge after cartridge into the rifle's magazine. Chambering a round with a snap, she looked at me.

"What are you waiting for?" she asked, as if nothing unusual had occurred. I kept my mouth shut and headed for the tree line.

You'll know soon enough what it means to step off the beach into the temperate rainforest. In most places like this, scrub trees, berry bushes, and towering devil's club choke the space between spruces and hemlocks. To travel in a forest with no trails is to battle one's way through a nightmare of confusion, whipping branches, and sudden, painful stumbles.

Breanne grabbed my coat as I entered the gray-green curtain of trees. She pulled me back, forcing in ahead of me, pushing the foliage aside with the barrel of her gun. Darkness closed around us as we pressed inward. My pack snagged on a broken hemlock limb. Yanking it free, I ran into Breanne, who had stopped abruptly. She listened. I listened, too.

Among the trees, the rain sounded different. It fell in a distant, quiet patter on the thick branches high above our heads. Only occasional large drops fell through the canopy.

Close to this sound, but different, came the whispers.

The voices, if that's what they were, spoke a language I don't know. I heard nothing I could understand, or repeat. Noise swirled about us, now nearby on our left, now distant, behind us, now far above our heads.

I turned to ask Breanne about it, but she had stepped away again, moving farther into the bush. The sudden distance between us startled me. Darkness and tangled brush made her hard to see.

She appeared to turn her head slowly from side to side. At one point she raised her rifle tentatively, then lowered it. The whispering grew louder, no longer blending with the rainfall. It grated harshly on my ears. I groped at my side for a hunting knife, my only weapon.

I lost sight of Breanne for a moment. Then I found her, even farther in the forest than before, looking at the ground. Suddenly, as I watched, she threw up her hands and began thrashing about in the dark, beating at the bushes around her. For a crazy second I thought she'd been engulfed in a swarm of black flies, but whatever happened here was far, far worse.

She must have dropped her rifle, because I couldn't see it, and she never fired it. I heard something else—a strange tearing sound. I will never know, but I'm afraid I heard her flesh tear away from her bones. I watched her die, unable to move myself to save her.

That's the last I saw of Breanne. As the whispering grew louder and clearer around me, I felt strong hands on my arms, plucking at my clothes, my pack, and hair. Something roughly removed the knife from my grip. I yelled, turned, and crashed through the brush in a panic.

Luckily, my blind flight led me back to the beach. I didn't know that until I collapsed on the rocks, slashing my hands on barnacles and mussels. Over my head, I felt a great rush, as if a flock of large birds—huge birds—swept out of the forest and across the water.

The whisper turned to a thunderous roar. A high wail mingled with it. I heard my sister scream in agony above me. I could not look up to see, but I was spattered with thick, salty copper drops from above. The sounds echoed against the mountainsides all around before fading into the night.

Search and Rescue picked me up a day later. They found me cowering knee-deep in the tidewater, muttering incoherently, staring at the tree line.

They searched for Breanne for weeks. They found a skeleton of a woman about her age. It matched Breanne's dental records, but the forensics team insisted, from the condition of the bones, that it had been out there for more than fifty years. They never found her rifle or my knife.

I have not been back to this beach since—until today. I wouldn't be here now if you didn't pay so well, and I didn't need the money so badly.

So, go ahead if you still want to, but I will not go into the forest with you. I'll stay here by the fire, with my rifle on my lap, watching to see if you come out again, and listening for the whispers in the trees.

SHELIKOF BAY

My father's eyes are a steely, storm-swept gray. Grandma used to say they reflected the gales that blew in from the North Sea to Kirkwall, where he was born. My mother said no, the storms in my father's eyes came from the mighty North Pacific, where it tore its heart on the rocks of Shelikof Bay, out a way from Sitka, the Russians' old capital in Alaska.

Mother used to stare at father's eyes, drinking in the gale-gray as if she thirsted for it, then look away, with a deep, ruddy blush on her fair face. My father stirred things in my mother that I was too young to understand. And my mother was a storm in my father's eyes and guts and heart and loin that tears and howls to this very day.

I know nothing of the North Sea's storms, as I have never gone to the ancestral home. I will always live in Alaska, my birthplace, and my mother's, so she said.

Mother speaks truly of Father's eyes. I have seen those storms. I was born on a night when one of them shrieked and shivered at the windows of our little cabin on the point, shouting to match my mother's cries and drown my own small birthing pipe.

That same year, Michael, the older son, ran his high-prowed skiff up on the rocks in Deadman Reach, in a crazy, desperate, fatal attempt to beach himself in an early autumn storm. They say he nearly made it, but in the end the wooden skiff looked like a pile of matchsticks. They didn't find Michael's body for days, having been thrown across the beach and into the deep tangle of devil's club at the forest's edge. The brother I never knew lies in Sitka cemetery, where my mother went often to mourn her child, until she went away.

Father told her, "Never mind, Girl. God only wanted us to have one son. When he gave us Ian, he took Michael away." Mother smiled at this, though I never knew why. It held little comfort for me, though I was the son God left them, but my mother's heart eased to hear the words. Mostly I think it was not the words, but the man saying them, that comforted her.

The days of our life played out like a song, full of beauty and hints of sadness, but playing on and on. I had hardly walked before I began to go with Father out on the ocean. I see him as he was then, with his hard hand sure upon the outboard throttle. I see his weathered, handsome face, silver mustache and shaggy hair, pipe clenched in his teeth, storm eyes squinting. We hauled crab pots and fished the waters, hunted the forest for deer and the high alpine meadows for grouse. Mother and my older sisters, Megan and Beth, tended the little cabin, growing a few brave vegetables, picking berries, taking in other people's laundry. In the winter, Father and I carved wooden figurines, and Mother and sisters embroidered. These things we sold to the tourist shops near the cathedral of St. Michael's, to bring in extra money. Simple, we were, and happy to be so. We worked hard, but we all liked it. Dangers were many, living close to Alaska's land and waters, but discontents were few.

Only, my mother would now and then stare out to sea from our little cabin, and sigh.

She was a woman of incredible beauty, fine features, auburn hair, and eyes big and dark and liquid brown. When she sighed, looking far and wild and away, my heart broke for her. Then I would run to her and throw my arms about her, even when I was older, and ought to have been shy of it. She'd catch me up and hold me, with the tiniest of sobs in her chest. Sometimes, when I opened my eyes, I'd see my father looking at her as if he'd been struck across the face.

Once she caught him looking, and something passed between them that was secret, helpless, and very, very sad. Then she smiled at him, a wicked smile, and he laughed.

Grandma came from Kirkwall to live with us when I was three. She cared for us on the few nights when Father and Mother would dress in their best and go to town. Then it was she would make up the fire, and bundling my sisters and me close in quilts, would tell us Orkney tales, of giants and faeries, standing stones and ghosts.

One night, when I was older, she told us of the selkie folk. We liked these stories, because there were so many seals to be seen near our home. We often saw them rise gently from the ocean, popping their heads up to calmly regard us as we passed. They have eyes of liquid brown, so much like our mother's. They would look, then slip silently under, like gray ghosts in a thickened fog.

Grandma said all seals were selkie folk, a race that fell from grace with heaven, banished to dwell in the sea.

She said they could slip their skins and be like us when they "got the land longin' on 'em." This happened in the spring, she said, on the seventh day of the spring flood tide.

Grandma sang us the song about the great selkie of Sule Skerrie, who made a baby with an island maid, and predicted his own death at the hands of the maid's future husband. She also told us of the young man who fell in love with a selkie girl, and how he captured her sealskin while she sat naked on the rocks, and made her his bride.

She told this story with a strange smile, and an odd flash of light in her eye, though it was only the sparkle of the fire.

The man and his selkie bride had many children, Grandma said. One day, one of the children saw her father oiling a sealskin, then hiding it in a chink in the wall. The child asked her mother about the leather coat she saw, and her mother, without a word, went to where the child said it was hidden, slipped it on, and disappeared in the foam.

It wasn't the saddest story Grandma told us on those long evenings, with the snow drifting and the waves hard upon the rocks of our beach. It touched me, though, and I promised myself to look for selkie girls on the seventh day of that spring's flood tide.

The gales rolled in one and another that winter, battering our little cabin and moaning like lost souls marching to hell. Many nights my Mother sat at our table, with the lamps turned low, staring out at the lines of foam skimming up our gravel beach as wave upon wave dashed in, driven by the crying wind.

My father sat in his chair by the fire, his hard fist curled around the bowl of his pipe, watching my mother. His love for her pumped out into the room with the rise and fall of his chest, and his billowing tobacco smoke.

Finally, he would ask her: "What are you thinkin' of, my Love?"

Most times she would reply, "Why, I'm thinkin' of you." Once, though, she answered, simply: "Michael," and another time, "Shelikof Bay."

When she said she thought of him, he would smile and sing her a song. Father had a beautiful voice, and would sing the old country airs in a voice like to calm the wild ocean.

But on the nights when my mother's answer changed, he would cluck his tongue and fall silent. Small and unobserved, I would watch them, and my throat would tighten and hurt from tears.

One morning in March, when Father and I came in with firewood, stamping the snow from our feet at the threshold, Father looked at Mother, sitting with her needlework at the window.

"If spring comes," he announced, "we'll go and make a camp at Shelikof." My mother leapt up and dashed to throw her arms about him, kissing his face all over. My sisters and I cheered, for we loved to camp. Grandma scowled, and predicted she would have to beg her good friend, Mrs. Haggerup, for shelter in town.

When the day came for us to go, Grandma took Mother's hand, and they walked together to the cemetery to visit Michael's grave. When we left our beach, Grandma held Mother close for a long time before she let her go.

Shelikof Bay is a wild place where the ocean rolls in to pound a crescent of sand guarded by rocks. Bears graze on the tall, green grass that grows between sand and dark forest. There's a cabin there now, but then it was an empty place, where no people seemed to go. How and why my parents knew it, I didn't know then.

After the tent had been wrestled erect in the lee of a rocky face, Father and I built a fire for his coffee and Mother's tea. My sisters raced about, discovering, followed by Father's gaze, sharp and gray, on the lookout for bears.

Mother, her hair and skirts teased up by the capering sea breeze, wandered barefoot close to the water's edge, beachcombing, dreaming. The sadness of the winter seemed washed away from her by the wind and crashing waves, making her beauty shine, her manner young and carefree. Father watched her as she went, his face drawn as if by pain.

That night we lounged by the campfire. Mother rested with her cheek on Father's knee, listening as he sang to make the forest hush and the sea rocks ring. He sang us *Over the Sea to Skye, The Maid of Orkney, The Black-Haired Lass,* and more.

He sang what we asked of him, but his face grew dark when Megan asked for *The Great Selkie of Sule Skerrie.* Mother sat up and watched him as he refused, then, with a mischievous smile, began to sing it herself in a voice that was strong and glorious. Father rose to his feet and, taking his rifle, tramped off into the dark.

When she had finished singing, we sat quietly for a time, listening to the fire spitting and cracking.

"I met your father on this beach, you know." My mother's statement surprised us from our secret thoughts. "He was here on a hunting trip, many years ago. I heard him singing one morning, and that was that. I fell madly in love, and no one else would do." She smiled at us, reaching to hug my sisters close. "Now, what do you think of that?" she asked, "Did you know your mother could be so brazen?" She laughed, and the sound was like the burbling of a stream bouncing over stones to the sea.

We had stayed at Shelikof Bay many days when a storm threatened, turning the sky yellow, then gray. The expectation of it was heavy in the air, but not so heavy as an expectation of another kind hanging over our camp. After breakfast, Father suggested he had seen a spring fawn and its mother at the far end of the beach. As my sisters and I left to explore this, I saw Mother take Father by the hand and slip into the tent.

Later, with the storm well on its way, and the open tent flaps popping smartly in the wind, Father watched the sky, its color matching his narrowed eyes. Then, clenching his pipe in his teeth, he strode to the tent. There he rummaged impatiently for a moment before returning, a rumpled bundle beneath his arm. Mother watched his progress, her features set. Father walked up to her and held the bundle in both hands before him.

"No," she said, weakly. Father matched her look, and firmly nodded.

"It's time, my Lovely," he said, "You've given too much of yourself now, and need to be takin' some for your own." He pressed the bundle to her, then crushed her to him, kissing her deeply. Beth, Megan, and I stood by, uneasy, not knowing what passed between these two. Then, he held her away, and liquid brown eyes searched gale-gray.

"In the spring, then?" my mother finally asked. Father nodded.

"The seventh day of the spring flood," he promised.

Mother turned to my sisters and me, giving each a long hug and many kisses. Then, with mounting excitement, she ran toward the surf, clutching the bundle in one hand, tearing away her clothing with the other, until she ran naked into the waves. She waded far out into the water, then shook the bundle loose. It was large and mottled gray. Pushing it into the foam, she stepped upon it, pulling one end up over her shoulders to cover her nakedness. Then, with a flip and a splash, my mother had gone, and I thought I saw, for just an instant, a fat seal sporting through the waves.

Father looked heartsick, staring out across the water. The storm hit full force, driving a cold, bitter rain into his face. Still he watched, until he allowed us to lead him up the beach and into the tent.

Megan had begun quietly to cry. Beth and I exchanged glances of wonder.

"Did you steal a selkie's coat, Father?" Beth finally asked. Father looked up, amazed.

"Steal—? Why, no, Girl," he said, his throat knot bobbing hard, "it was she who came to me. I, a silly lad fresh from Orkney, and here she was, the most beautiful woman, standing naked in the Alaskan surf, holding out to me a fine seal pelt."

His voice failed him, and he sat, miserable, silent, as the storm came down about us and had its say.

MOTHER IS A SELKIE

Father's eyes are haunted now, staring across the foam
Searching for the deep brown eyes of his lady love
My mother
Fairest woman found in these rain-swept islands
My heart cries out to her
As her heart cried out to the sea
She loved us
She loves us still
But a wild thing must return to its home
Father is a strong, good man
Mother is a selkie.

CHILDREN OF THE FOREST

I never used to be afraid of the dark. Even as a small boy, I ventured bravely into the night, never worrying about what might be hiding in the gloom. That changed in the winter of my twenty-third year, when Robert Calldellin told me of the little people.

We stood on Robert's porch at his place out the road. We talked about fishing, watching the early afternoon dusk come on. Robert was describing the halibut rig he planned to purchase, when he stopped mid-sentence. He stared into the forest that edged his property. I heard him sigh strangely.

Without a word he turned and entered the cabin. I looked at the darkening woods, trying to discover what had arrested his attention. Robert returned with his hunting rifle, took deliberate aim, and fired into the bush. Lowering the weapon, he stared hard again, then quietly swore.

I had known Robert for about ten years. I'd call him steady, not one to take potshots from his front porch. His property sat close to the road, making his action illegal, and Robert meticulously followed the rules. I couldn't imagine why he would fire his rifle there.

I began to say as much, when, without looking away from the forest, he grabbed my arm, pulling me backward toward the front door.

"Come on," he said, "it's getting dark, and we could use a drink."

We huddled in his small kitchen, warming our hands on mugs of hot coffee laced with whiskey. Robert had locked and barred the front door when we entered. Now he fidgeted, looking everywhere but at me. Questions consumed me, but I kept quiet until, at length, he spoke.

"Funny thing about Southeast Alaska," he said, "how your eyes can play tricks on you." He stopped, seeming to judge this a bad start. A moment later he tried again.

"There are little people in the forest." Apparently, he had settled on the direct approach. "I don't know what they want, exactly, but they're dangerous."

"Little people?" I asked. Robert's Gaelic last name conjured images of leprechauns.

"Children," he said, "sort of. I first started seeing them about a year ago, when I was in Gimcrack." Gimcrack Canyon was a dreary, moss-hung crevice a day's trailless journey into the mountains of our island. A thin trickle drained it, feeding a sunken muskeg pond, brooded over by ancient, twisted cedars. It was Robert's preferred deer hunting area.

Robert had stalked a buck, finally bagging it in the early evening. As he dressed it out, the ceiling lowered to the treetops, and a steady rain began falling. Robert decided to make camp. He had no tent, so he constructed a lean-to of hemlock boughs. Soon he had soup simmering on a small fire.

Robert camped away from the dressed-out deer in case of bears. As darkness fell, he began a circuit to gather firewood, checking the deer on his return. All seemed well.

As he approached his fire, Robert thought he saw a pale figure flit away from his shelter. Running forward, he found his rucksack spilled on the ground. A quick inventory showed a few food items missing. Alarmed, he fueled his campfire, then sat with his rifle across his knees, keeping watch.

Two hours later he had seen nothing, and his wood supply needed replenishing. Reluctantly, he went out looking for more.

"By that time everything was soaked," Robert told me. "I searched beneath old growth to find dry wood under the roots. I was spooked, so I grabbed extra before heading back to camp. When I got to where I'd hung the deer, it was gone."

"Bear?" I asked.

"I thought so, but the signs said different. One rear hock remained, and the skin of it appeared to be scratched by claws too small for bear."

Robert guessed a wolverine stole the kill, although the strange markings didn't match that animal. Robert returned to camp.

Flames leapt up as he fueled his dying fire. Glancing up, Robert saw glittering eyes and a pale form in the trees across the pond.

"It was the face of a child," he assured me, "or of something the general size and shape of a child. I only saw it for a moment as it glared at me, then vanished."

Frightened and exhausted, Robert settled into the lean-to, trying not to think too hard about what he had seen, or the loss of the deer.

Several hours before dawn, Robert awoke suddenly.

"I dreamed or sensed a presence in the lean-to," he said. "I felt someone hovering over me, but when I opened my eyes there was no one there." He took a long drink of his whiskey and coffee, his eyes tired, his expression drawn.

"That's when the screaming started."

A high-pitched wailing rose around him. Unnerved, he scrambled from his sleeping bag and looked outside.

Slight, pale figures encircled his camp. He could barely see them in the gloom, as they stood some thirty feet from him.

They looked like emaciated children. Many had long, stringy hair as pale as the rest of their bodies. They created a chorus of wailing and screaming as they circled his camp, hands linked.

"It was nerve-shredding," Robert confessed. "I've heard the death screams of dozens of animals. In the first Gulf War I heard fighter jet attacks and close-range bombing. None of those had the effect on me this noise had!"

As he watched, Robert groped for his rifle, not daring to take his eyes off the circle of figures. He found it, chambered a round, then crept out of the lean-to.

"I didn't like the idea of them coming at me from behind," he said. "I stood up in front of the shelter, giving myself a clear view. These things," he said, fortifying himself with another generous slug of his drink, "were humanoid, but not human." They were very slight, with tiny hands whose pointed fingers suggested needle-like claws. Their mouths were wide, "like frogs or something," he said. They had sharp, tiny teeth—lots of them. Instead of noses, they had thin nostril slits. Their eyes looked like black holes.

"I don't know how long I stood there, listening to their screaming," he said, "but finally, they made their move."

With alarming speed, one of the beings broke the circle and dashed in at Robert. He was so surprised, despite expecting just such a move, that the creature passed him and returned to the circle before he knew it. A long, thin gash appeared across his left hand.

"It felt like I'd been burned," he remembered, unconsciously rubbing his hand as he spoke. I saw a thin, white scar.

Seconds later, another figure dashed in, slashed at Robert, then retreated. Soon a line of creatures moved forward. Robert, in a panic, shouldered his rifle and began firing almost indiscriminately at the white shapes as they darted past.

"I hit a few," he told me. "Others rushed in and snatched the bodies away immediately." When they started dying, the screaming, which Robert had thought could get no worse, heightened in pitch and volume. The urge to drop his rifle and cover his ears almost overpowered him.

"Bear in mind," he told me, "I was firing my .30-.30 as fast as possible—it's loud, but I could hardly hear it over the shrieking." Luckily, his steady rifle fire soon sent the creatures into the forest. Robert found himself alone in Gimcrack Canyon.

As soon as he caught his breath and controlled his panic, my friend gathered his gear and left, hiking out through the dark to escape.

"I barely made it," he told me, his face pale at the memory. "They followed me. I could see them flitting from tree to tree at the edge of my vision the whole way home.

"Since then, I've learned how dangerous they are. They scared me the first time, but it was only the weirdness of it then, not the knowledge of real danger."

Robert had gone hunting again, in an area far from Gimcrack Canyon, to which he never returned. His enthusiasm waned considerably with the discovery of the "little people." He spent so much time shooting at them when they appeared around him in the woods, he had little chance of finding game. The few times he did bag a deer, they usually robbed him as they had in the canyon. On this trip, about nightfall, an incredible sound nearby startled him.

"It was like a moan, but full of changes and..." he hesitated, groping for the right word, "...textures. At times it rattled or gurgled, and it wavered from high to low at irregular intervals. Now and then it changed to a full-throated roar. Blending with it was the scream of the little people!"

Curiosity overcame Robert's fear. Making his way stealthily forward, he found a muskeg clearing, where a huge brown bear stood at bay, encircled by the wraith-like little people.

"That bear was scared," Robert said. "I've seen frightened bears before, but this one was out of its mind!" Robert soon found out why. The little people began their dashes, rushing in one at a time, at amazing speed. Some lashed out with their little hands, others darted in to bite the bear with their needle teeth.

"The bear began screaming," Robert shuddered. "The amount of blood was terrible. It towered above the creatures, and you know how thick a bear's coat is. Still, they slashed it to ribbons in minutes. It never had a chance. Then they started eating...."

We fell silent for a time, my imagination working to create the scene, Robert's apparently struggling to block it out.

"They've gotten braver," Robert half-whispered. "They come at night fairly often now, to scream outside my cabin. Once, I shot one inside!" He pointed to the wall behind me, where a rifle slug had ripped a hole.

"Why haven't you mentioned this before?" I asked. Robert regarded me with hollow eyes.

"Would you have believed me if I told you?" he asked.

"I'm not sure I believe you now," I confessed. His gaze shifted to somewhere behind me, then back.

"Look quick."

He suckered me. I whirled around. Through the window at my back, I saw something slip away. It appeared to be a pale child. I glimpsed an evil expression on a moonlike face.

I screeched and upset my coffee cup. We both jumped up. I grabbed a dishcloth to mop up the spill. Robert grabbed a rifle from the wall rack. Checking the lever action, he handed it to me and went to get shells.

"Did you drive or walk over here?" he called.

"Walked."

"Then you'd better stay here tonight," he said, reappearing. "Not that you'll get much sleep," he flashed a wan, sickly smile. My hair stiffened and my neck tingled as I loaded the rifle.

We waited. The winter night, which fell as Robert's incredible story unfolded, pressed close. We turned off the lights and squinted out the windows.

"I'm not sure what we're supposed to be doing here," I admitted.

"Believe me," Robert said heavily, "when the time comes, you'll get a pretty clear idea of what has to be done."

He was right.

I had almost begun to nod off in spite of my fear, when a thin, high wail rose from the stillness outside. It came from every direction, seeming to include sources inside the house. It began as a single note that fragmented into remarkable dissonance, filling the night with nerve-jangling sound. Robert murmured something like "get ready," then a pale figure flashed past my window. The panes in front of me fell away, silently, it seemed, although the sound must have been drowned by the ear-piercing shrieks. I looked down to see blood spilling across my hand where glass shards had cut it.

Before I could look up again, a searing path cut across my forehead. Hot blood poured into my eyes. I panicked, grinding at them with my fist, trying to clear my vision and level the rifle at the same time.

I heard gunfire behind me. Through the blur, I saw Robert firing through the window on his side of the house. My ears rang from the shots and the rising howl outside. My eyes closed against my will, stung by the flow down my face, blood mixed with sweat. I struggled to keep them open, desperate to see. My life depended on it.

I fell back from the window just as a thin, ghostly arm snaked across the sill toward my face. I fired—wildly—my bullet smacking into the wall above the window, but the arm instantly disappeared.

"It works better if you aim at them," I heard Robert remark dryly. I screamed a string of obscenities at him as I wallowed in the broken glass scattered among spilled rifle cartridges on the floor. His fresh volley of shots, and the incredible banshee din of the little people, drowned out my hysterics.

I struggled back to the window, thrust the muzzle of my rifle through it, and fired rapidly. Each time I emptied the weapon I fell back, scooping up handfuls of cartridges and glass from the floor, hardly feeling the pain in my fingers as I jammed the blood-slick rounds into the magazine. A few times, as I fired, I saw the quick flash of a pale figure dropping, and others darting in to bear it away. This faint realization that I was killing some of them gave me courage.

Until they started dropping from the ceiling.

I don't know how they did it, or when, but suddenly I heard Robert yell as needles raked across my back. The room exploded. I choked on acrid smoke. Robert shot one of the creatures as it fell on me from above. There was no time to absorb this, as I saw Robert fire in the air. Looking up, I saw the little people skittering across the ceiling like giant, pale spiders, to drop on us. I flopped on my back and pumped bullets at them, then managed to scramble up to cover the unprotected window again.

A vision appeared out of the dark. One of the little people loomed up, eyes like pits, wide, frog-like mouth rimmed with horrid, needle teeth. I felt like I was trying to raise a thirty-foot log instead of a rifle barrel. It came up achingly slow as that horrid face flashed closer. I knew I was going to lose my nose, at least—if I was very lucky. The gun seemed to go off by itself, apparently from someplace under my chin. Too close, I watched the creature fall, saw others retrieve it immediately.

I thought morning would never come. I didn't think our ammunition would last. To my indescribable relief, as pale light finally dawned, the little people faded into the forest. A long time later I realized their screams had died away as well. Finally, convinced it was over, I slumped on the floor, unmindful of the glass and blood. My skin burned from a thousand slashes.

My breathing slowly returned to normal. I dropped the rifle, not even bothering to eject the round in the chamber, and turned weakly to Robert.

My friend stretched facedown on the floor under the shattered window. His body was horribly sliced and bleeding. He looked like he had run through a razor-wire gauntlet. I crawled to him and turned him over. His one remaining eye stared at the bullet-pocked ceiling.

That's exactly how the police found us.

Ironically, there is no insanity plea in the state of Alaska. I didn't even try to tell what had happened. I spent my effort convincing my lawyer to help me in other ways. As I cowered in Juneau's forest-surrounded Lemon Creek Correctional Center, he arranged for my life sentence to be served in an urban institution, far from Alaska.

Joliet is well lit until lock up. Pale pastels and prison blue are a comforting contrast to the dark greens and deep grays of my former home. People constantly surround me. The smell of their cigarette smoke and sweat screen me from any whiff of verdant Alaskan rainforest that might somehow drift to me on a northwest wind.

And yet, in my dreams, I see the pale, pit-eyed, frog-like faces darting up out of the black. I hear the high-pitched wail of the children of the forest in my cell, in the laundry, over the wall in the yard, in the crowded mess hall.

And I am very, very afraid of the dark.

MORLEY'S DREAM

Wish fulfillment through dreams, dream interpretation, and astral projection were all hogwash to Morley Washburn. He believed dreams were merely the subconscious mind at play, unhindered by rational thought, largely free of conscious control. He did not place any significance in his nighttime visions. Even so, about once or twice a week, Morley's mind made a nocturnal drive up a certain road, headed for the tourist shop, quite literally, of his dreams.

Morley dreamed of taking that road on a sunny afternoon. The road seemed unfamiliar to him, which was strange. Born and raised in Juneau, he knew every inch of the city's limited road system, public and private. Logging roads strayed for miles through backcountry around other Southeast Alaska towns, but this dream road he traveled was different: as broad as any street in Juneau, well paved, with guardrails on the steeper stretches.

Despite seeming odd to him, Morley had the distinct impression, in his dream, of finding something long forgotten. Driving the road felt comfortable yet exciting. It seemed as if he had always known of the road, but had taken far too long to remember the way.

In his waking hours, his dream eagerness to drive the road amused him. The road took an impossible route in the real world. It started in downtown Juneau and went up Mount Juneau, which rises abruptly—in many places vertically—some 3800 feet above the city. There is no physical way the road could have been cut into the mountain at all, much less with such a gentle grade. Still, whenever he visited it in his dream, the landscape made perfect sense.

When Morley chose a college to attend, he decided on San Diego State University. Like so many Alaskan youths, he longed for a complete change from the life he had known. He met, dated, and married a classic southern Californian beauty. By the time the marriage ended, so had his desire to live "outside."

The dream had begun its occasional visitations in his sophomore year, slowly increasing frequency through graduation. The dream hadn't prompted him to move back to Juneau, although it did come more often once the decision had been made. After he returned to Alaska, the frequency increased again.

Morley's anticipation grew as he drove the dream highway. He rushed back to a barely remembered place, anxious to arrive. Even so, quite often he would pull out at an overlook that provided a spectacular view of Gastineau Channel. The pullout was guarded by two stern totem poles, somehow foreshadowing, for Morley, what would come. Each time he dreamed of that stop the monuments pleasantly surprised him. He was well versed in northwest coast Native art, and very likely knew every standing pole in Southeast Alaska, but he always recognized these dream poles as new to him. He never went close enough to examine them thoroughly, noting only one figure, identical on each pole: a man or boy with two faces. Always, he found himself back on the road, heading toward his destination.

The phantom highway didn't end at the strange little tourist shop. Morley "knew," as one does in dreams, that the road continued across Mount Juneau, eventually entering the Lemon Creek area. It didn't matter, because his journey always ended when he pulled up to the shop.

He never knew the name of the place, a low-slung, glass fronted wooden building painted pale green, with cedar shake roof. A massive Haida totem graced the entrance. Morley's dream self assumed it had been collected from one of the Queen Charlotte Island villages in Canada, judging from the girth of the huge tree from which it was carved. He always stopped to admire the pole before entering the shop.

As he opened the door, a little tattoo of greeting beat on an instrument hung above the inside door handle, a little round drum with two or three marble-sized beads suspended over the head. Small bells sewn around the rim of the head made faint musical accompaniment when the motion of the door set it playing.

Morley usually found himself alone in the shop. Sometimes he would dream of an odd-looking proprietor, a spare little man who greeted him from behind the counter. He wore a gray shop apron over a banded collar shirt. He was balding on top with a fringe of long gray hair that produced two preposterously swept tufts on either side of his head. His sparkling eyes appeared huge behind thick-lensed "granny" glasses. Whenever he appeared in the dream, the strange fellow would welcome Morley, then retire abruptly through a doorway behind the counter after inviting his visitor to explore at his leisure.

To Morley's great delight, the store held much that had interested him since his youth. Northwest coast Native artifacts of every size and description filled shelves, cases, and floors. He browsed among skin drums and bentwood boxes, carved wall screens, horn ladles, model canoes, hats of wood and woven cedar root, argillite trays and amulets, masks, Chilkat and ravens-tail robes, pre- and post-contact weapons, halibut hooks, rattles, and totems of every size. He also found fossils: mammoth tusks, ammonites, trilobites encased in dark slate, and skulls of saber tooth cats. He wandered for hours through this dreamscape, pleased to find that everything had a price, and it all, from the most common to the most rare, fell well within his means.

Morley welcomed this happy dream whenever it came, and thought of it during his waking hours. He often awoke from it to find himself searching his bedclothes for a particularly exciting purchase, just as he, as a child, used to search for toys he had dreamed of in the night.

The dream had one disturbing aspect. He was always convinced, while dreaming, that the road through the mountain and the little tourist shop actually existed. When he awoke, and his conscious mind took over from the unconscious, he realized that wasn't true. Even so, a small suggestion remained that the place did exist, waiting for him to remember it, if he only could.

Eventually, Morley decided to try to alter the progress of the nocturnal journey.

Despite dismissing the significance of dreams, he knew they could be manipulated to a certain extent. Almost every time he dreamed of a compromising situation with an attractive woman, something held him back, reminding him he was married. To his great annoyance, this restraining voice continued even after the divorce. Every great once in awhile he found the power to tell himself it was a dream, or remember he was divorced. Then the activity progressed as he wished. Couldn't he, then, will a change in his recurring dream?

He began to focus on what he wanted from the dream, hoping that if and when it returned, he could affect a change.

What *did* he want from the dream? Very little, really. He mainly wished to study the details of the totems at the overlook. He wanted to read the name of the curio store, and remember more details of the merchandise. Perhaps, if possible, he would ask the shopkeeper a question or two, should he appear.

Ultimately, he wanted to put at ease that small part of him that thought the place really did exist, after all. Were these such monumental changes that he couldn't will them? Morley wanted to find out.

He might have been more successful, initially, if he studied the subject. The growing new age movement offered plenty of instruction books. Morley didn't care to hear this advice. He felt a dream, as a product of his unconscious, could be ruled by his own will without outside help.

Soon enough, he found an opportunity to put this theory to the test.

He dreamed himself driving up the road on a pleasant afternoon. Low sunshine shouldered past patches of overcast to the southeast, illuminating the edges of silver-gray clouds. A gentle breeze ruffled the roadside weeds, combing through the high grass and scrub alders on the shoulders and slope of the road bank. Warm in the sunlit cab of his pickup, Morley knew it was cool outside. His favorite old sweatshirt lay on the seat beside him, ready to be pulled on when he reached his destination.

A flash of blinding light reflecting off water warned him of the approaching overlook. Silhouetted against the channel far below, twin totems stood, featureless in the glare. As he often did, Morley slowed and turned into the pullout on the down-mountain side of the road.

His shoes crunched on the gravel-strewn pavement. A sudden gust buffeted his rig, tousling his hair, trying to pull the door from his hand as he pushed it open. Without looking back, he snagged his sweatshirt. Putting it on, he stepped toward the totems.

Delighted, Morley realized he was manipulating the dream, then immediately tried to forget it. Dream manipulation, he felt, is a Zen exercise: one must do without doing. Think too hard about anything, and one risks awakening. Let it happen, but will it to happen as you wish. These thoughts flashed, then faded, as he moved back into the dream.

The poles, as he could clearly see, were a matched pair. They were almost identical, like a set of house posts might be, but these he guessed to be free standing memorials. He judged them to be Tlingit, but after carefully, lovingly examining each carved character, decided they weren't modern. He could identify the work of several noted contemporary carvers with a fair level of confidence. These weren't the work of the Beasley brothers, nor were they Jackson, Wallace, Peck, or Brown. They appeared weathered, but not too old. He guessed they might be careful reproductions of older poles.

He searched his memory for images from old photographs and drawings, but found nothing to compare with these two poles. He admired the craftsmanship for a long time, soaking in the details.

Each stood about 20 feet high, dominated by five figures: a raven at the top, a killer whale below, a wolf, a human figure with two faces, one on each side of its head, and a man pulling apart a sea lion—Duktoohl, the legendary Tlingit strong man.

At length Morley ended his guessing game, looking for a plaque that might explain their origin and meaning. He found none. Well enough, he decided.

He looked again at the poles' human figures. He recalled seeing a photograph in a book of a similar carving of a boy with two faces. The author speculated briefly that it represented an actual person, since no legend survived to account for it. Upon consideration, Morley found it rather interesting to see this second representation of the rare piece.

After admiring the totems a bit longer, he turned to look out over the channel and the small glimpses of Juneau in sight before returning to his vehicle.

Shortly, he rounded a curve in the road where it began a slight descent. There he found the shop, guarded by the great Haida post. He didn't have to look for the name of the place. The name "North Country Traders" was obvious on the sign above the door, gold gilded black letters on a brick red background. Why couldn't he read it before?

The drum hanging from the door clattered as Morley entered the store. The building was well heated by the low sun through the glass front. Dust roiled and danced in the shafts of light streaming down on the glass cases and their contents. He stood alone, but hardly noticed—his attention focused on the details of the room.

The inventory had improved since his last "visit." Several brand new totems stood against the walls or by the wooden beams holding the rafters in place. Their unpainted surfaces glowed, indicating fresh yellow cedar.

On one countertop a display of silver bracelets sparkled in the light. He picked up each in turn, examining their etched figures.

He wandered for long minutes, gazing, touching, and trying all kinds of interesting artifacts and fossils. At length, a spare figure appeared in the doorway.

"At last, you've come!" the man exclaimed. Morley hardly had time to wonder at the comment. Gray tufts bouncing, apron fluttering, eyes bright, darting, and huge behind bottle-bottom lenses, the little man bustled forward and shook Morley's hand warmly in both of his.

"Call me Simon," the man said. "Yes, yes, my, my, my!"

He seemed overjoyed to see Morley, who in turn felt suddenly shy, taken aback. "Make yourself at home, my friend," Simon continued. "Get to know the place. What's mine is yours!" he exclaimed, and laughed so hard he had to pull off his thick spectacles to wipe them on his shirtsleeve.

Trying to ignore this, Morley continued to peruse the contents of the shop. His wandering gaze fell upon a figure on the counter, the carved wooden figure of the two-faced boy, the very one he had seen in the book.

♦ ♦ ♦ ♦ ♦

Few people noticed the changes in Morley Washburn. If he seemed not to recognize them on the street, or failed to turn when they called his name, this wasn't so unusual. Morley had always been the distracted type. Banded collar shirts were somewhat in style, so his sudden preference for them seemed unremarkable. Hairstyles change, often with little or no comment.

An acquaintance or two may have noted his new interest in local events, and the relish with which he drank in Juneau's architecture. In a time when people could and did switch often between contact lenses and spectacles, no one commented on his new glasses, the lenses of which were as thick as bottle bottoms.

NONE BUT THE DEAD

Olaf Hedricksen stepped from the dinghy to the gravel beach and surveyed the stillness, tin coffee cup in hand. A refreshing offshore breeze, almost bracing, carried the scent of forest, muskeg, and morning. It made a gentle rushing sound, coaxing answering sighs from the forest as it moved among the boughs. A raven tolled the hour with echoing croaks. Hedricksen fingered his pocket watch from his vest for confirmation. It was coincidence, obviously, but entirely satisfactory.

He savored the steam from his coffee for a moment longer as it mixed with the cool, salty air, then tossed the dregs. Pitching the empty tin cup over his shoulder into the boat, he gestured to his crew.

With great strides he made toward a row of massive wooden monuments and warehouse-sized buildings lining the top of the beach. Less enthusiastically, warily even, his men followed him toward the deserted Haida village.

A few steps later they stopped, muttering among themselves. Hedricksen turned, questioning. One of the men cleared his throat uneasily.

"Skeletons, Cap'n," he said, pointing.

Hedricksen and his crew were "collectors," raiding coastal towns for stored-up treasures. They plied their craft with impunity, virtually free from interference from authorities. In fact, they were financed and patronized by some of the most honorable and prestigious institutions of learning in the United States and Europe. Their crimes, underwritten by the world's museums and universities, were committed in the name of anthropology, because the people they preyed upon were Native.

Hedricksen justified their work by targeting only "abandoned" villages. He knew that by raiding in summer, when whole towns migrated to seasonal fishing and hunting camps, they were sure to find even the most populated coastal settlements standing empty.

True, conditions on the northwest coast might lead one to believe its villages were deserted. Cedar, the primary building material of the indigenous civilizations, weathered quickly. The region's lush vegetation thrived in the extended summer daylight. Even an active village might seem about to be reabsorbed by the northern rainforest. Men like Hedricksen knew better, but feigned ignorance in the name of profit.

"Skeletons, y'say? What the hell are you talking about, Morgan?" Hedricksen grinned. "You children have been telling ghost stories on watch again."

"No, Sir," Morgan objected. "Look, Sir." Among the forest of totems towering at the edge of the beach, carved wooden panels topped some shorter poles like signboards. From behind several of these Hedricksen saw something hanging loose, stirring in the breeze. Looking closely, he made out a limp skeletal arm, a mostly decomposed leg or two, some wisps of decaying hair.

Stepping forward, Hedricksen pulled a revolver from his belt. Taking aim, he shot a bony hand off the nearest pole. The crew flinched and stepped back, murmuring uneasily. Several of them crossed themselves hastily.

"You're a bunch of women," Hedricksen growled, stowing his smoking pistol. "Let me teach you something about these Indians. They bury their rich folk in those posts, and sometimes, as the posts rot, the dead get loose. You'll see worse before we're done. It ain't pretty, but it's no concern of ours. If you can overcome your superstitions, we can get some work done. There's none but the dead to stop us from making our fortunes today." He watched greed rally their faltering courage.

"Spread out," he barked. "Morgan, you take Janns and Merriweather. Start at that end of the village. Molly, Horst, and Gregg take the other. Check the lodges. Bring out anything carved or woven, especially fringed blankets, copper shields, and cedar chests. The rest of you check those totem sticks." He pointed out some of the better specimens. "I'd guess those there, and that one over there will be worth cutting down. We'll take the two best. Give a shout if you find anything made of gold or silver." He glared at them for a moment before finishing.

"Get at it, and no more pissin' your pants over skeletons!" He turned and continued up the beach as the crew hurried to work.

Hedricksen surveyed the area. The look of this village suggested it really was abandoned. Likely there had been smallpox here. The disease had recently torn up and down the coast from Vancouver to Alaska, a plague among the Natives, exterminating or dispersing whole settlements. He judged this to be a rich one from the number of totems. If he'd had a more seasoned crew, they could pick the town clean. No matter. These whelps hired in Port Townsend would do well enough. If the place really was deserted, he could make another run before winter, if profitable.

He walked among the huge houses in an improved mood, enjoying the silent morning, occasionally poking through the grass for discarded items of value.

Sun shining through high haze warmed the day. Silvered cedar house planks reflected the heat and added subtle fragrance to the sea air.

Hedricksen removed his wool cap to let the breeze play through his dark curls. Wandering around behind a nearby house, he stopped short.

Here, as in many villages, the bodies of dead slaves and less distinguished citizens had been deposited in the open to be absorbed by the forest. Most of these remains had been scattered, reduced to skeletons, further evidence the town had been empty for some time. The discovery also confirmed what the mortuary columns indicated: the missionaries that traveled the coast had not influenced this village. One of the first changes these ambassadors of God and white civilization attempted was more sanitary treatment of the dead. Not that Hedricksen cared about the Natives' welfare. His concern was that conversion might have led them to destroy their artifacts, as had been done in many Christianized settlements. Missionaries were simply bad for business.

A sound caught Hedricksen's ear. At first he thought it was one of the crew, but it was pitched too high. It was a song. As his mind oriented to the possibility, he heard it more clearly. Someone—a woman—was sweetly singing a beautiful melody.

It came from somewhere behind the village's single row of houses.

Hedricksen scowled. A woman's presence would doubtless mean men as well. He drew his pistol and began to search.

The forest started a few feet behind the rear walls of the houses. Several openings, overgrown with coarse, high grass, led into the trees. Selecting one, Hedricksen followed it, stepping over whitened windfalls in his path. His boots sank into wet sod as he encountered muskeg, the peat bogs of the northwest coast. Choosing his steps carefully, he made his way to a clearing, where he found a small pond. What he saw there made his heart race.

A Native woman, faced away from his approach, bathed in the water. She appeared to be young, her skin clear and smooth, her back muscular and well formed beneath a shower of glossy black hair. As she stood, singing and splashing water over her shoulders, Hedricksen admired the curve of her waist and tight posterior, enjoying a peek at ripe breasts whenever she turned even slightly to the side. He caught his breath at what he glimpsed when she bent toward the water.

This was a rare spectacle for a sailor in this part of the world. Women were scarce here and always properly, if not warmly dressed. Even the few prostitutes found in larger white settlements often kept most of their clothes on while plying their trade. Native women either dressed like the missionaries or were dirty enough, by white men's standards, to disguise the beauty so many of them possessed. Hedricksen felt extremely fortunate to happen upon such a shapely, clean, nude Native woman.

Cautiously, he moved forward. The maiden appeared to be alone, yet showed no fear of being discovered. Her song seemed to have no words, but the tune was more melodic than the traditional, rhythmic Native chanting that Hedricksen had heard and disliked. He stopped at the pond's edge, lowering his pistol, entranced by the vision before him. Finally, sensing his presence, she turned.

Her striking eyes were clear and dark, her high-boned cheeks flushed from her bath. Her face was free of tattoos, and no labret, indicating a highborn woman among these people, protruded from her plump lower lip.

She regarded Hedricksen calmly, her luscious mouth turned up slightly in a faint but welcoming smile as she continued to hum her melody.

Hedricksen stood frozen, fixating on the swell of her perfect breasts. His fascination seemed to amuse her. She thrust her chest forward subtly, allowing him the most advantageous view.

He noticed the decoration she wore. A medallion hung in her décolletage from a simple leather thong. He recognized the material as argillite, a black local slate that was becoming a lucrative trade item. Somewhat larger than a dollar piece, it was intricately carved in the totemic style perfected by the Haidas. The carving's central figure, a face, featured inlaid abalone shell eyes that contrasted sharply to the dark stone.

Hedricksen spoke a greeting in Chinook trading language, his voice hoarse with desire. She smiled and shook her head slightly, indicating she didn't understand. He knew no Haida, and was momentarily stumped.

Then she moved.

Water ran in tiny rivulets from the valleys and secret places of her body as she emerged from the pond. She stepped close to him, looking up into his eyes, splaying her slender fingers across his broad chest. Parting her lips slightly, she slowly lowered her gaze, becoming demure. Language would not be a barrier, Hedricksen decided.

He folded her in his arms, kissing her deeply, thrilled by the softness of her skin, cool from the water yet warmed by the blood rushing beneath its surface. He had never held—had never *seen* a woman this beautiful. Circumstance heightened his pleasure. He would not have considered sex a possibility when he awoke that morning, had he thought of it at all. Now he crushed this desirable creature to him, and she responded with a hunger that seemed to match his own.

At length, they lay close together on the heather, spent. Well satisfied, Hedricksen pressed his face against her, smelling warm, clean skin. He kissed her throat gently as his hard sailor's hands kneaded the flesh of her round derriere. She rolled to face him, kissing him deeply.

Hedricksen suddenly realized it was late afternoon. Their love play had dulled his sense of time. Had he dozed? He ought to see to the men. Who knew what they might have found by now and perhaps hidden away to sell on their own? He rose, reaching for his trousers. The girl made no move to stop him. She watched with an amused expression that puzzled, but did not concern him.

When he had dressed she came to him, speaking again in her own language. She removed her medallion and put it around his neck. He examined it closely for a moment, admiring the craftsmanship. Surprised, he realized he had considered keeping it for an instant before estimating its worth to his patrons. Even so, he pulled a thick silver ring from his finger and presented it to her with a smile.

He turned toward the village. At the clearing edge he looked back, but she was no longer there. He scanned the area for a moment, then shrugged. She was an Indian, after all, he reasoned, skilled in stealth and woodcraft. He strode off to check on his men.

The village was as silent as they had found it that morning. Hedricksen crossed from the forest edge to the row of houses, surprised to see the Native remains had been cleared away. Some among his crew were Christians. Perhaps they had collected the bodies for burial. He hoped this had been done after they had selected the best totems, carefully cut them down, and transported them to the ship. If not, Morgan and the others would hear from him. Sentimentality is fine, as long as profits are assured first.

Hedricksen stood at the edge of the gravel beach. No one else was visible. The dinghy floated at anchor, having been overtaken by the rising tide. He could see no evidence of work on the totems. No stacks of goods waited to be hauled to the ship. The scene remained unchanged except for one large bentwood cedar chest laying open in the grass, and the absence of the corpses they had seen hanging out of the mortuary columns.

Hedricksen became livid. Expeditions of this sort were costly and not without risk. There could be no excuse for wasting a whole day.

"Morgan!" he bellowed, "Merriweather! Gregg! Horst!" He heard no answer but the cackle and caw of ravens perched on silent totems.

"I'll flay your skins from your backs!" he roared. "Show yourselves, dogs!" Hedricksen glared from house front to house front, unable to comprehend the lack of response.

Far down the row of houses, a figure emerged from an entryway cut into the base of the huge cedar monument decorating the building's facade. Hedricksen hurried forward, squinting to learn the man's identity. He stopped short as the figure pitched in the dirt and remained still. Had he seen an unnaturally thin arm push the body from behind?

Fear suddenly gripped Hedricksen. Casting wildly about, his eyes fell on his Haida lover, standing beside one of the larger totems, watching. She smiled in the same peculiar way she had when she watched him dress. Her lovely, full lips parted, and she began to sing.

At first she sang the clear, sweet song that had drawn him to her, then, subtly, she changed it until it became a rhythmic chant.

Aghast, he watched as the bloom of her skin faded. The woman's complexion creased and cracked like old hide. Her shimmering fall of ebony hair frayed and grayed, becoming a tangle of dusty wisps, like a mass of cobwebs in a neglected rafter. In a matter of seconds, as she continued to chant, she mummified, becoming a standing corpse. Her bony jaw dropped, and she laughed in a dry, rasping cackle.

Hedricksen, frozen in place, stared horror-stricken until the leather thong that held the totemic medallion she had placed around his neck snapped tight, breaking his spine.

THE RAVEN CALLS AT DAWN

I'm sitting near a window in a corner room of an old stone hotel in Harlowton, Montana. Evening is coming on, and a storm sweeps across the high plains from the Crazy Mountains southwest of here as if rushing to greet the coming darkness.

My hand rests on a bottle of tequila, which I have brought up from the saloon downstairs. Beside the bottle is an old Colt revolver, which is useless except for momentary comfort against that for which I feverishly scan the land in front of me. Closer at hand is an object at which I can scarcely bear to look, although I believe my life depends on it. My tired eyes strain for any movement in the brush outside, watching for the thing that drove me to this tiny Montana town, the thing that made me leave the home I loved so desperately for so long.

As I search I reflect on the implications of confronting mythology. It does something to a man's mind when legends become reality, when that which has always been regarded as fictional suddenly proves to be terribly real.

Consider Bible stories. By definition they are stories, whether one believes them to be fact or fiction. People told each story, filtering reality through points of view, sets of belief, and intentions until it arrived, inevitably changed, to the printed page. There it is read and filtered through the reader's mind. At that point who can judge how closely perceived reality resembles true reality? When we at last stand face-to-face with God (if I will be so lucky after what I did a few nights ago) I imagine our Biblically based preconceptions will be stripped away and we'll find that God is really quite different from what we believed Him to be.

I've been thinking a lot about meeting God lately, as it's quickly becoming clear that it is my only remaining hope. I'm convinced the thing I'm watching for is going to catch and kill me. Like that future meeting with God, my encounter with the kushtaka stripped away all the stories, leaving me confronted by a horror I had never known.

♦ ♦ ♦ ♦ ♦

Northwest coast Native cultures tell of a race of land otter people. There are many different legends about these mysterious inhabitants of Southeast Alaska, called *kushtaka* by the Tlingits, and *gageets* by the Haida. The white people, supposedly "superior" to such superstitions, have had their share of encounters with this unknown entity. Some of what I had heard about the land otter people was Native legend, but much of it was told by white people, diluted by imperfect recollection, differing cultural orientations, and embellishment.

An intriguing explanation of their existence came to me directly from a Native elder in Angoon. He said the kushtakas were some of the few remaining Neanderthals that kidnapped women from the camps of Tlingit ancestors during their prehistoric journey across Beringia, through the interior of Alaska to the southeast coast. In my ethnocentric superiority I decided this must be where the story began, and that all else was the embellishment of subsequent generations.

I was dead wrong. That is, if the creature I encountered *is* a kushtaka, then it's something more than a Neanderthal, unless our ancient cousin possessed the powers of teleportation, invisibility, and shape changing.

It began on a hunting trip in Thomas Bay, near my home, Petersburg. The bay is traditionally known as the home of the kushtaka, although I never found out whose tradition that was. People told strange stories about the place, but they also said the hunting could be good there, so that's where I went.

I tramped through the area for two days without finding any deer. I hadn't seen wildlife of any kind, which I found a bit discouraging, but not strange. Something was there, as a shrill, piping whistle could be heard occasionally in the surrounding brush.

Each evening I returned to my campsite on the beach. I'm not a superstitious person (or wasn't) so I had no trouble sleeping at night. I kept my Winchester '94 loaded by my side as I slept, but that was more for bears than bogeymen. I awoke each morning to an undisturbed campsite and found it the same each evening.

Late in the afternoon of the third day I negotiated a patch of devil's club, cursing my luck and deciding to give up the trip. Several thorns caught in my leg, and the tips had broken off in my skin. I was in for a lot of pain. If I was lucky I could get them out, probably not until long after I'd returned home.

I finally worked my snagged pant leg free and stepped into a small clearing. Flustered and hurt, I glanced around to get my bearings and discovered another person there with me.

It was Sandra Livingston, a woman I'd had a relationship with some years before and hadn't seen since. She was tall and slender, with short red hair. I was completely surprised to see her standing there, watching me with her hands jammed into the pockets of a hooded sweatshirt, but it didn't seem *too* strange. She was an outdoorsy type, and I'd met people in the forest before on occasion, even people I knew, once or twice.

The fact that it was Sandra threw me. When our affair ended she left me. I had stayed in love with her for a long time afterward. I thought I'd gotten over her, but seeing her like that, especially in such an unexpected situation, sent an electric thrill through every part of me, leaving me staring with my head swimming and my jaw slack.

She watched me silently with a mild expression on her face. I continued to stare until I became embarrassed, then collected myself enough to favor her with a bashful grin. As she smiled back her lips parted, showing teeth. Not *her* teeth, but teeth like long, sharply pointed daggers, a mouthful of them!

I staggered backward into the devil's club from which I'd just extracted myself. At the first prick of the spines I stopped short, brought up my rifle, and without thinking, fired at the figure's head. I didn't hit it. With a shrill whistle, it vanished in a puff of vapor.

It had all happened in an instant; it took longer for my mind to absorb it. For the first time since coming to the bay I thought of the kushtaka legends. I vaguely recalled they could appear in any form they chose, particularly as their intended victim's loved ones. One supposedly recognized them as supernatural by their teeth, which, if I remember correctly, were iron.

The sabers I saw in this creature's head weren't iron—they had gleamed like the finest ivory. It was a minor point, one that I was unwilling to stay and ponder. I ran through the forest toward my campsite as quickly as I could.

Night fell as I made my way, neither making my passage easier nor comforting my mind, which raced much faster than my body could. When I finally broke free of the woods, I galloped headlong down the beach, gaining more momentum than my feet could handle. I crashed into my tent, collapsing it under me. Good enough. Gathering it in my arms, I threw it in my skiff. Two armloads of gear followed. It wasn't everything, but it looked like I could live without what was left.

I dove into the stern of the skiff, wrestling with the outboard motor while shoving the craft away from the beach with one foot. I looked back once at the tree line—only once. On this rare, clear night a full moon had risen during my flight through the forest. My glance at the trees showed the silhouette of a large timber wolf, its breath smoking in the cool air. If it was the thing that had been Sandra transformed, I didn't want to know. With a silent, fervent oath and a hard yank, my motor started, and I escaped.

Heading back to Petersburg from Thomas Bay in an open skiff at that time of night was a stupid idea. It would have been bad enough if I'd made a calm, rational decision to do it. In my present state of mind it invited catastrophe, but I was well beyond thinking. I pushed the motor hard, speeding blindly over the water with only the full moon for light. I should have been watching the surface for snags, but my eyes locked on the high, pointed prow of my skiff.

Even so, I doubted my vision when I saw two dark, clawlike hands come up on either side of it. An instant later a large, hairy body hoisted itself over the prow into the skiff. I cowered in the stern, barely able to control the outboard.

The thing was short, with muscular arms that seemed longer than mine by a good foot. I expected it to attack immediately, but instead it hunched down in the bow and turned to watch the water ahead. At short intervals it turned to glare at me with eyes that seemed to glow red in the moonlight and mutter angrily in words I couldn't understand.

When it turned back, I found the courage to pick up my rifle. I raised the weapon, aimed carefully at the base of its neck and fired.

I know I didn't miss. The beast whipped around, bared its huge teeth and let out a howl that raised my hair. With a powerful leap, it flew up and over the side of the fast-moving skiff, disappearing into the water with a huge splash.

I had been running the outboard almost full throttle to that point, but I gave it what was left and made a quick jiggle toward the side the thing had gone over, tensing for the jolt I hoped to feel as the prop sliced the submerged body.

Nothing happened. I continued at high speed until I calmed down enough to realize the danger of my situation. Throttling back to a safer speed, I made my way home.

I lived in a little house near the Presbyterian Church. Safely inside with doors and windows locked, I began to feel secure. Fear and exertion exhausted me, and it was well past two o'clock. I fell on my bed and slept peacefully until late in the day. When I awoke the whole adventure seemed to be considerably less real. I began to think it had never occurred.

Any doubt vanished that night. I had been asleep for hours when I awoke to the sound of very light tapping, almost like the ticking of a warm house as it cools in the evening. I thought that's what I heard, but it slowly, gradually grew louder. It didn't come from one place, but sounded like someone rapping lightly on every pane of glass in the house.

I lay in the dark listening, sorting sounds, trying to detect accompanying noises that might provide a clue to its source. I wondered if friends were playing a trick on me. Finally I found the energy and nerve to get up, dress myself, and investigate. Memories of the events in Thomas Bay prompted me to reach for my rifle as I went.

I don't know why I didn't look out my bedroom window instead of walking through the house to the front room. Maybe I hoped to avoid whatever it was for as long as possible, yet still make myself think I was doing something productive. As I went the tapping grew rapidly louder until it sounded like fists beating on the glass. I chambered a round, swallowing hard. The sound became deafening. I went to the window and reluctantly pulled back the curtain.

There was nothing there.

More precisely, I could *see* nothing there. Something beat on the glass. The panes vibrated visibly and the noise was incredible. I went from one window to the next, searching but finding no one responsible for the pounding. I began to fear the glass would break.

Summoning my courage and brandishing my rifle, I went out the front door. The noise was only slightly less terrific outside. I circled the house twice without finding anything. I stood on the front porch once again, perplexed, when the pounding ceased abruptly.

The silence was almost more unnerving. As I turned to go inside, the skin of my neck began to crawl as if I were being followed. Losing my courage, I rushed inside, slamming the door in panic. Resting against the closed door, I became aware of a burning sensation on my back. At the same time I felt dampness on my spine where it pressed against the wooden door. I felt my back gingerly, pulling back fingers wet with blood.

My blood.

I ran to the bathroom. Through a series of contortions I managed see my back in the mirror. My shirt had ripped cleanly in half. A long, deep, very straight scratch started between my shoulder blades and ended short of my tailbone. It looked as if a long claw had swiped down my spine. I shuddered from the sting and the sudden memory of the claws of the beast in Thomas Bay.

Four hours later I boarded a state ferry headed for Wrangell. I had suddenly rationalized a visit to my friend, Lucas Jimmy. If anyone could tell me about the kushtaka, Lucas could.

I wandered the ferry nervously, clinging tightly to my battered daypack. It held an old Colt revolver and two boxes of shells—very illegal, as all firearms are to be checked with the purser upon boarding. I wasn't letting go of it. I considered it a poor substitute for my rifle, which I didn't imagine, even in my panicked state, I could smuggle aboard.

The pack also held clothes, food, and credit cards. I didn't want to admit it but I was on the run. The pounding on the windows wouldn't have done it alone, but the scratch that burned and itched when I moved convinced me it was time to leave. I didn't have a clear plan; I just wanted to get out of Petersburg for a while.

I found Lucas at Shakes' Island in Wrangell's inner harbor, where he worked with a crew restoring some of the local totem poles. When I suggested to him that I had been chased by a kushtaka, he dropped his carving tool and laughed until I thought he would be sick.

"So, White Man, you got the bogeyman after you, huh?" he finally gasped. "What makes you think our spirits give a shit about you?"

"Hell, Lucas, I don't know!" His laughter and the unwelcome interest of the other carvers embarrassed me. "You're the one who told me all that stuff when we were kids. It might be Bigfoot for all I know, or Jimmy Hoffa in a gorilla suit."

I told him all that had happened. He stopped laughing and returned to his work as he listened. I could tell by the set of his brow he thought hard about what I told him, although he tried not to show it.

I finished and stood in uncomfortable silence, furtively checking the reactions of the other carvers. Their responses ranged from complete disinterest to consternation or fear—even anger—to open derision.

Lucas stayed quiet for a time, throwing his energy into his carving. Finally, without looking up he said simply, "You need to talk to my grandmother."

"Right," I smirked, "you want her to laugh at me too? If she laughed as hard as you did, she'd have a heart attack!" An extremely uncomfortable pause followed, in which everyone in the yard stopped work to stare at me. Lucas glared for a moment before his expression softened.

"You must not have heard, Man. My grandmother already had a heart attack. She died four months ago."

Mortified, I began to stammer an apology, but Lucas smiled and waved his hand in dismissal.

"My fault, Buddy," he said. "You couldn't have known, and I was the one who made it sound like she was still around. Let's go get something to eat." He carefully stowed his tools, and we left the carving yard. I went willingly, still blushing from my gaffe. I could hear merry laughter from the other carvers when they thought us beyond hearing.

The Jimmys owned a snug little house near City Market. On the way in I stopped to admire a newly completed house post leaning beside the front door. Lucas was a talented carver, and his skills had improved considerably since our last meeting.

When we entered I got warm hugs from Lisa, Lucas' wife, and their young sons, Michael and Walter. We locked my pistol in Lucas's gun cabinet, and they made me feel at home. Soon we were eating Lisa's famous lasagna. For the moment we had no more talk of kushtakas, and I began to feel better.

♦ ♦ ♦ ♦ ♦

It's getting dark. It's harder to see the prairie outside the window of this old stone hotel. Now and then I see movement but it's mostly the wind disturbing the sage. I'm not used to tumbleweed, but they're pretty obvious as they roll from place to place so they don't concern me much. I watch a house cat skulk by, probably after ground squirrels.

The tequila is beginning to calm me, but I'm careful not to become too complacent. I shouldn't worry—I think I'm too scared to get really drunk.

I wish it were morning. The night is going to be much too long.

I ring the front desk and arrange for a coffee maker to be brought to my room. When the desk clerk comes I'm careful to conceal my pistol and the other thing. I don't want any more trouble than I already have.

♦ ♦ ♦ ♦ ♦

When Lucas returned to work he pointed me toward the public library with a list of titles to check. I spent the afternoon studying Tlingit and Haida legends without getting much from it. I learned that kushtakas "saved" drowned people by transforming them into their own kind. Most of the stories told of drowning victims who used their newly acquired supernatural powers to help their living relatives. That seemed pretty benign.

The only potentially useful information I found was a mention of sharpened dog bones being effective against kushtakas, and that they needed to be "gone" each morning before the raven calls. It wasn't much, but by the end of the day I eagerly grasped at even the most vague information.

Walking back in the evening I thought I heard one shrill 'peep' emitted from a grove of alders between two churches. Suddenly I recognized the noise, possibly because of my musings in the library. I had heard two different animals make that sound. Marmots call warnings with a similar whistle. So do land otters. I heard this same noise in Thomas Bay—the same sound the creature made when I shot at it the first time! I quickened my pace, anxious for the safety of the Jimmy home.

"Sharpened dog bones?" Lucas asked, skeptically. "Could work. Then again, garlic may drive off a vampire." He leaned forward in his chair to look me steadily in the eye. "I appreciate your faith in my people's mythology," he smiled, "but you've got to realize we're dealing primarily with a bogeyman here—a monster parents told their kids about to keep them out of the forest at night. I think it's pretty much the same as the witches and werewolves your European ancestors told their children about—pure folklore."

"How can you be sure?" I asked. "They say there's an element of truth in every legend told, so someone must have run up against a creature like the one I saw at least once before."

"Sure there's an element of truth," Lucas snorted, "the truth is just what I said: stay out of the woods.

"But suppose you're right, and there *is* a kushtaka. I wouldn't bet my life on help from a dog bone or an early rising raven." He grew serious. "I really wish you could talk to my grandmother. She would have known what to say to make you feel better. She knew the old ways, and they make a lot of sense, but she could have told you what was real and what wasn't.

"One more thing," he warned me. "What I've told you here is only my opinion. A lot of people take the kushtaka very seriously—so seriously that they won't even discuss it, and they get very nervous, even angry, if anyone else does, especially a white boy like you! Best keep this to yourself."

The Jimmys put me in a little guest bedroom upstairs. I slept peacefully, imagining the kushtaka or whatever it was couldn't have ridden the ferry with me to Wrangell, despite the noise I imagined in the alders.

That belief shattered in the night, when I was jolted awake by the most frightening shriek I'd ever heard. It was unbelievable—sharp, high pitched, so loud it seemed to come from inside my head, and completely, utterly inhuman. Even roused from sleep, my fogged mind immediately rejected the possibility it could be Lisa or the boys. It was wild and earthy and unmistakably evil. It froze me so thoroughly I couldn't draw breath. It turned my stomach, nearly making me ill where I lay. It became a continuing howl, rising and falling above the frantic shouts of the Jimmy family outside my door. That got me moving, pulling on clothes with violently shaking hands.

When I get chills from the flu, there comes a moment when I stop trying to fight the shivering, and give in to it till my whole frame rattles. That's how I shook as I dressed. I turned to the door, but it flew open in my face. Lucas reached in and grabbed my shoulders, pulling me out into the hall. The whites of his wild eyes gleamed in the dim light.

"Get *out!*" he choked. "You've got to get out *now!*" He slammed a hard object against my chest. I grabbed the pistol as he hauled me back into the room to get my pack.

"That thing is in the house!" he hissed, "If it gets my family..." he let the thought trail off, turning to me. "We'll face it together if we have to," he said, "but you *must* go. The ferry you came in on got delayed. It's at the terminal right now. Get a ticket and leave."

He pushed my pack at me and pulled his own pistol from the waistband of his pajamas. Inanely, I wondered how the elastic had supported such a heavy piece. Then we headed downstairs, weapons ready. The howling had not abated for an instant. As I passed the last doorway I glimpsed Lisa and the boys huddled miserably in a corner. She held a very large hunting knife uncertainly before her. Her eyes betrayed no hint of rationality.

"I'm sorry," I managed weakly as we clambered down the stairs and into the kitchen. What we found there drew us up short.

The whole room was literally in pieces. Cupboard doors hung open—not by their hinges, but panels slashed apart by long, sharp claws. Shards of wood, punctured food containers and broken glass littered every surface.

We made our way across the wreckage as the kushtaka appeared in the doorway. It looked much as it had when it climbed aboard my skiff, but standing erect, focusing its glowing red eyes on us with obvious deadly intent it was even more frightening than it had been.

I heard Lucas whisper a disjointed prayer behind me as we both raised our guns and shot wildly at the beast. It crouched and charged, sending us fleeing through the house and out the back door.

"Go, go!" Lucas shouted. Slipping on the wet boardwalk, struggling to keep my feet under me, I ran as hard as I could across the yard, through the gate, and down the street toward the ferry terminal.

Do you have the same dream I have? Do you dream you are pursuing someone, or being pursued, but you can't see properly to do it? You panic because something veils your sight, preventing you from doing what you must. This dream became reality for me as I sprinted through Wrangell's streets. The town is fairly well lit but dark alleys along the way make it hard to see. The light blinds dilated eyes, which in turn can't penetrate the next stretch of darkness. I knew these streets fairly well a long time ago. I had seen some changes in them on my daylight walk to find Lucas, but the night and fear transformed them into an alien landscape.

The abrupt transition from sleep to frantic exercise nauseated me. I wondered what had happened after I left the Jimmy house. I had visions of my friend Lucas lying bleeding to death in his own backyard, ripped open like his kitchen cabinets. Pushing the scene from my mind, I adjusted my pack and increased my speed.

I tried to listen for following footfalls above the roar of blood in my ears. My mind showed me the silhouette of the huge timber wolf at the Thomas Bay tree line. Could the thing be speeding to overtake me on canine paws? The edges of my sight began to swim in dark purple clouds. Overexerting myself, I began to hyperventilate. I feared I would faint.

I slammed hard into the ferry terminal door. It jarred enough sense into me to make me shove my pistol into my pack before entering.

The man who sold me a ticket must have thought I was crazy or drunk, sweating and panting, wild-eyed as I paid. The timing was perfect—I could board immediately, as the ferry was just ready to cast off and depart.

Another agonizing rush upstairs and out onto the deck, where I crouched behind a hanging lifeboat to watch the gangplank for my pursuer. Had it slipped aboard while I gained my vantage point? Was it invisible? I clung to the railing, half swooning until we were underway. Then, staggering to a lounge, I crumpled in a corner to sleep.

♦ ♦ ♦ ♦ ♦

It's night now. The storm hits, making it hard to see through the blowing rain. I wonder vaguely if there are ravens in Harlowton to call at dawn, to bring me relative peace. I wonder if I'll be alive to hear them. One hand brings my coffee, heavily laced with tequila, to my lips. The other hovers between my pistol and the ivory shaft beside it, one representing safety from the known, the other from the unknown.

◆ ◆ ◆ ◆ ◆

When I awoke I took a quick inventory of my person and belongings. The gouge on my back continued to heal well, although it caused a good deal of stiffness, especially after sleeping on deck all night.

I dug out my ticket to see where I was headed. Of only two possibilities, I hoped for Bellingham, Washington but I read Prince Rupert, British Columbia as my destination. That would mean passing through Canada—not necessarily a bad thing, but I needed every advantage I could find, and being outside the U.S. didn't seem like one.

By the time we reached Dixon Entrance I felt fairly satisfied the creature hadn't gotten aboard the ferry. I felt more at ease as I stood at the railing, watching the ocean and the passing land.

Dixon Entrance is one of my favorite places. It's the gateway to Alaska, my native state. Looking at the mountains north of the entrance could be bitter or sweet, depending on whether I traveled south or north. Now, as I watched them recede, sorrow overcame me. I had become a refugee. I felt I might never return home. My cheeks stung from tears turning cold in the wind. I stared hard as the Alaskan shoreline slowly disappeared in the mist, trying to remember every detail, hoping to imprint a vision of it to stay with me no matter what happened.

Entering Canada proved extremely tense. Handguns are strictly forbidden in that country; bringing one in is a serious offense. When the customs agent in Prince Rupert asked if I carried any firearms I looked at him levelly and lied. Luckily, he didn't search my pack.

I hitchhiked east from Prince Rupert on the Yellowhead Highway. I made slow progress—not many people wanted to give me a ride. I don't blame them. I can imagine how I looked as I peered at each driver, searching for relatives or friends or the hairy face of the kushtaka itself behind each steering wheel. The resulting expression couldn't have inspired confidence in anyone who saw it.

When evening came I wandered off the highway, crossing the Skeena River to the village of Gitwangak. I carried a reflective thermal blanket, and had purchased a wool one in Prince Rupert. I would keep warm if I could find a bit of shelter. I strayed down the road by the river where a row of weathered Tsimshian totem poles stood. After recent events the sight of these poles lifted my spirits, despite reminding me of the presumed nature of my pursuer.

Carved wooden monuments like these were one of the chief pleasures of my Alaskan life. I stopped to look before it grew too dark, feeling as refreshed as if I had drunk cool water at the end of a desert trek.

Several of the poles had deteriorated quite badly. One had a large wolf as a base figure. Examining it closely, I found a hole the size of a silver dollar in the carving's forehead. To my surprise, a white bird appeared from inside the hole and chirped at me. It was missing one eye; the other looked milky, as if afflicted by a cataract. The bird was blind. I couldn't understand how it survived, since it wasn't very far off the ground and there must have been cats in the area. I welcomed the distraction this puzzle provided, and thought hard about it as I continued down the line of poles.

A pack of dogs joined me. They swarmed around as if in greeting, allowing me to pet them as I spoke to them. Their rough appearance and lack of collars suggested they were at least partly feral. That they practiced pack behavior became obvious when one of the larger dogs pressed in close to have his ears scratched. A smaller dog with a graying muzzle and well-scarred brow took offense, snapping and growling. Immediately the larger dog cowered in the grass as the older one snarled over his head, baring well-worn teeth in a show of superiority.

We played for a while before walking through the tall grass behind the totems to find a place to sleep. When I'd selected a spot and spread my blankets, the dogs huddled around me. I welcomed them, deciding the added warmth and companionship they provided justified the risk of a few fleas or ticks. Shortly, we slept.

I think I actually felt the dogs' tension before waking to their growling. They lay about me completely alert, looking toward the heavy brush bordering the river. The grizzled leader stood, ears laid back, teeth bared. I could see nothing, but fumbled for my pistol and a box of shells, cursing myself for not reloading after the encounter at the Jimmy residence.

As I fed bullets into the cylinder the other dogs jumped to their feet, mimicking their leader's menacing stance. A few of them began to inch forward uncertainly. Mingled with their growls I heard a low hiss. It didn't sound like a cat—more like a very large weasel. It seemed to come from the brush line. I hoped it might be a wolverine or a lynx, but as much as I tried to deny it, I felt convinced it was the thing that had pursued me in Alaska.

Pistol ready, I rose shakily to my feet and peered at the brush, trying to make out shapes or movement. The dogs became increasingly excited, until at length the alpha dog rushed forward, leading the pack into the bushes. I hesitantly stepped forward but stopped as noise burst from the foliage.

The dogs attacked something that fought back viciously. I could hear bodies being thrown around in the thicket. The barking, snarling, and snapping of the dogs mixed with yelps and sharp whistles that had become all too familiar.

It occurred to me that if dog bones repelled kushtakas, perhaps a whole dog or two would do the same job. I certainly felt willing to hang back and let them tear the thing apart. From the sounds I heard, that seemed to be their intent.

A sudden loud, high-pitched cry trailed off into a keening lament, then silenced. My curiosity overcame my fear; I moved forward to see. As I broke through the brush line I saw a dark, upright figure melt and lower into a four-legged shape and sprint off through the woods, pursued closely by the dogs. I started to follow but stopped short before a motionless figure in my path.

A friend often teased me for my tenderness toward pets. I cringe at the mention of dog-eating cultures, while he points out that any animal is pet or food, depending on one's point-of-view. His mother, he told me, had a pig for a pet. She judged it a better companion and playmate than any dog she owned. She loved it, but eventually her father butchered it, as originally intended. She said it was difficult, but she did eventually eat it. He warned that a time might come when my life would depend on killing and eating a dog I loved.

Such talk made me miserable, and he knew it. I recalled my friend's pragmatism as I stood over the lifeless body of one of the dogs that had befriended me. In the fight with the creature the sharp stump of a broken sapling had impaled my new friend.

I listened to the fading sound of pursuit through the bush, thinking hard. Finally I walked resolutely to my daypack, pulled out my sheath knife, and returned to the body. I had to work quickly before guilt overcame me. I also determined to be well finished by the time the other dogs returned. I didn't want them to see me do what I felt I must.

♦ ♦ ♦ ♦ ♦

The storm has passed and the high plains are quiet again. In the darkened hotel room I can see through the window clearly. Nothing moves on the prairie. Despite coffee and fear, I feel my eyelids wanting to close. I glance at the bed behind me. It looks very comfortable. It seems so long since I've rested properly, but I don't dare fall asleep. Not if that thing is out there.

♦ ♦ ♦ ♦ ♦

The dogs limped back before dawn. I had cleaned up my mess and buried the dead dog before falling into an uneasy doze in my blankets. They muttered and whimpered as they snuggled close. I looked them over as well as I could in the dark without disturbing them. I saw gashes and missing tufts of fur on muzzles and shoulders, but none of them seemed to be badly injured.

They settled, but remained fairly alert. I felt better, but guiltily shooed their inquiring noses away from my pack.

At first light they roused me as they grew active. I petted and talked to them, examining their faces for smears of blood, which might mean they had injured or killed the kushtaka. The dried blood I saw appeared to be theirs. To my relief, their wounds were minor and would likely heal quickly. Packing my gear and scratching them all behind the ears once more, I hiked back to the highway as a raven, perched atop one of the old totems of Gitwangak, cackled at the dawn.

By the time I reached New Hazelton, I'd decided. I couldn't risk flight on foot any longer. I found the railway station and bought a ticket. On a whim I abandoned my plan to cross as directly as possible into the U.S. I decided to see the country in grand style, and purchased a bedroom to Toronto. I would cross over at Niagara Falls and maybe go to New York City. There seemed little chance of encountering a kushtaka there.

I had time before the train arrived, so I found a secluded spot and set to work. From my pack I pulled a bone about ten inches long. It gleamed white and clean after a wash in the river that morning. I began to carve with my sheath knife—difficult work, as the bone was still wet and new, but before the train came I had whittled a sharp point with a fairly keen edge on each side.

If a sharpened dog bone would kill the thing, I had a weapon in case it still pursued me. I breathed a brief blessing for the dog that had died in the night. This was a poor way to treat him for his help against the creature, but I wanted to live, and would pay the price to do so.

Traveling through Canada by rail wasn't the thrill I'd imagined. Apparently I'd had too many thrills lately. That evening I sat hunched over a cup of coffee in the dining car. The steady noise of the train comforted me with its constant reminder of mechanical power, but it also lulled me dangerously close to sleep, which I feared even while speeding cross-country.

"I don't believe it!" said a very familiar voice. I froze when I heard it. A tall, slender woman slid into the seat across from me, leaning over the table to catch my eye.

"Well," she said, "aren't you even going to say 'hello?'" I couldn't—I could not make any sound. Sandra sat before me, smiling the smile that stirred me so deeply every time I saw it. This time, though, I felt stirrings elsewhere inside me as I stared at the kushtaka sitting well within striking distance.

Her expression faded, replaced by a puzzled look when I failed to respond, then changed again to knowing amusement.

"I'm sure you never expected to see me here," she said.

It said.

"Last you heard I was in Florida, right? I'm coming back from visiting my mother's best friend in Jasper, and couldn't resist a long, romantic train ride to the east coast. So, how are you? You don't look so good. You're not doing drugs, are you?"

The question angered me, momentarily taking the edge off my fear. There was enough of Sandra about this thing to do that. I played along to give myself time to plan.

"No," I croaked unconvincingly, forcing a wan smile. "I'm just really tired. Things have been...strange lately." I slurped too much coffee to keep from adding, "as you well know." Her brow puckered in genuine concern.

"I'm sorry to hear that. Anything you'd like to talk about?" She actually reached across to touch my hand.

It was her touch. Soft and warm, it electrified me as it always did, whether she brushed past me in the kitchen, or made love to me. I began to feel dizzy. I had to assume this was the kushtaka, imitating Sandra perfectly in order to snare me.

I desperately wanted to believe it really was her, and that she had experienced a change of heart toward me, as it appeared. I needed the comfort and safety of her arms, to pour out to her the whole story of the nightmare I'd been living.

However, I'd prostrated myself once before, when she left. I would not do it again, even if all hell pursued me, and she offered my only hope. Her hand continued to rest on mine, warm and reassuring, stroking ever so slightly....

I steeled myself. My survival depended on remaining absolutely focused. I concentrated on the hurt I felt when she left. I summoned the anger, the sense of betrayal. I thought of the long, slow recovery—what recovery? I'd *never* gotten over her, and now she thinks she can sit down at my table and continue as if she'd never left? I smoldered, but controlled my feelings even as I dredged them up, to avoid betraying my intentions to the kushtaka.

I lied glibly, making up a story about someone new, someone *better*, I implied. Someone I'd loved more than anyone else—but she died. I quickly warmed to the narrative, dragging it out with long, humorous descriptions of our life together. As she listened, as I composed the tale, I kept track of the time, waiting for it to grow late.

♦ ♦ ♦ ♦ ♦

It's too dark to see, which is fine. My eyes aren't focusing anymore. My mind buzzes from the caffeine and alcohol, and from memories parading before me. I find the courage to glance down at the piece of bone by my pistol, to pick it up and stare at its whittled point and edges until my vision blurs with tears. It's sharp enough to do the job. It was sharp enough to cut out my heart.

♦ ♦ ♦ ♦ ♦

Eventually I led Sandra by the hand to my private sleeper, where my story continued. As she listened she played with her hair, which had grown longer since our last meeting. She leaned forward with a gentle smile, always keeping eye contact. I knew this behavior very well. It meant she wanted to make love. I fought against the urge to take her face in my hands and kiss her by concentrating on the story, which by now seemed completely preposterous to me, but which held her attention nevertheless.

Finally, I excused myself and went to the lavatory. I leaned against the sink in the tiny cubicle, staring at my reflection in the mirror, searching for any sign of the courage I would need in the critical moments ahead.

"It's not Sandra," I told myself quietly, "Sandra dumped you, and there's no way she's changed her mind after everything we said. She's not here—it's the kushtaka, and you have to kill it before it kills you!"

It wasn't much of a pep talk. I fortified it with more recollections of the pain I had felt when Sandra left. I had to build a bloodlust if I hoped to succeed. I had to bring out that darkest part of the psyche we all hide away and deny, the part that wanted to kill her for leaving. It was the only way I could drive myself to destroy this thing that looked, acted, even *smelled* like the woman I loved.

I returned, my passions aroused to the point I could do what was necessary. She stood with her back to me, leaning against the window, looking into the blackness. I couldn't ask for better positioning. I slipped a hand into my pack, silently pulling out the sharpened dog bone and a T-shirt.

Before she could turn around I rushed forward, mashing the shirt against her mouth to muffle her screams, pressing the point of the weapon into the top of her left breast. I bore down hard, as if trying to drive it through her body into my own chest. She struggled briefly, then to my utter astonishment, fell limp and bleeding to the floor with a thin, rattling exhalation.

I had expected something very different—a puff of vapor like before, a transformation to the kushtaka's real appearance, or perhaps some other form. I expected anything but the dying woman before me, which forced the immediate conviction that this really was Sandra after all. I had just murdered Sandra! I collapsed beside her, unable to grasp the incredible set of coincidences that brought her, of all people, back into my life at this fatal juncture. It was unthinkable—unimaginable, yet irrevocably true.

I fought the onset of shock, hurriedly gathering my wits. Pulling the bone from her breast, I wiped it off and jammed it deep into my pack. I quickly pulled out some clothes: sweatshirts, jeans, and a denim jacket. I tied a pair of pants thickly around each knee, put on the jacket and wrapped my elbows in sweatshirts. I secured my pack tightly to my back, checking to make sure it wasn't loose anywhere. I bound the remaining sweatshirt around my head, making sure my ears were well covered, and yet I could still see through a narrow slit.

Carefully stepping over Sandra and the incredibly large pool of blood, I found the emergency release tabs on the window and pressed them. It pushed out and away, held by hinges at the top of the panel. I squinted into the wind, watching the terrain that rushed toward me.

I waited until I saw a patch of lighter color, which hopefully meant level ground, then scrambled out the window before I could reconsider, pushing away from the outer wall of the train car as I fell.

I hit the ground before I was even sure I'd left the windowsill. I had planned to defuse the impact of my fall by rolling, but had little success. I landed hard, bounced, crashed, then sprawled, dazed.

I remained still for a long time, crying in pain, frustration, fear, and most of all, guilt. I passed out or slept, exhaustion overcoming my sense of self-preservation.

I opened my eyes to darkness. I looked around without moving my head, extremely stiff and afraid to discover how badly I'd injured myself. I lay in tall grass that seemed to conceal me from whatever might be nearby. Slowly I experimented with different muscles until at length I felt confident I had no broken bones or sprains. Bruised and sore, I had survived. I suddenly remembered the dog impaled on the broken sapling, and shuddered violently, visualizing myself in that same position by the railroad tracks.

I began to think my luck hadn't run out after all. Then I remembered Sandra. I scrambled to my hands and knees, pulling the sweatshirt from my head in time to vomit forcefully.

I found it inconceivable that I had taken Sandra's life. That I had done so under such strange circumstances, believing I'd killed the kushtaka in her form, made no difference to me. I doubted it would make a difference to the Royal Canadian Mounted Police, either.

I scarcely had time to dwell on this. I had sunk to a prone position again, resting my face in the sweatshirt. I would gladly have stayed there forever had I not been jolted into activity by a sharp, barking squeak in the near distance. I felt I lacked the physical or mental strength to defend myself, but I rose to my feet unsteadily, feeling in my pack for the dog bone. Pulling it free, I brandished it before me in a defensive posture and slowly circled, searching the darkness.

I had steeled myself for a swift attack, leaving me completely unprepared for what finally came.

As I kept my nervous vigil a mist formed along the ground and slowly crept forward to envelope me. I wasn't even aware of it until it grew thick around my ankles. I felt a chill beyond the cold of the night, and looked down. I couldn't see my feet through the dense fog. It rose quickly, my panic rising with it. As it reached chest level I felt as if an icy hand or paw clutched my heart, squeezing to stop its beating. I turned frantic circles, slashing blindly at the air around me.

As the mist rose to the level of my throat I felt a coarse-haired, clawed hand close on my windpipe. As the powerful grip tightened on my throat I stabbed with the bone knife, driving it hard toward my own Adam's apple. An awful shriek filled my hearing, joined instantly by my own as the chokehold loosened. The beast's scream turned to a howl as it retreated. The mist instantly vanished, leaving me alone by the railroad tracks, shaking and bleeding, scared witless, but alive.

♦ ♦ ♦ ♦ ♦

I've lost my courage. Quickly, trying not to be seen from outside, I draw the curtains and turn my chair to face the door. My fingers trace the scabbed-over wound at my throat. For the thousandth time I ask myself if I am mad. Could it be the kushtaka exists only in my imagination?

I rise and shuffle to the bathroom to examine myself in the mirror. The gouge left by the pointed bone is quite clear. Only a few very faint marks beside it might be bruises from the hand of the beast. Just as easily, they could be marks left by jumping from a moving train. I stare hard into the eyes of my reflection, doubting my own sanity.

♦ ♦ ♦ ♦ ♦

When the eastern sky grew light, I strained to hear the call of a raven. I still had no idea if a kushtaka truly had to be "gone" before then, or where they needed to be gone to, or for how long, but the dog bone seemed to have saved me in the night. Perhaps that meant the other restriction also held sway. It gave me a sense of security at any rate, and in my position I needed all the security I could muster from any source.

A raven flapped down from a stand of willows and croaked hoarsely before sorting through the roadside gravel for some unknown thing. I felt the tension between my shoulders release, and walked a bit more easily. I had gained some measure of confidence earlier by changing under cover of darkness, burying my bloodstained clothes in the brush.

When I reached a small town truck stop I borrowed a first aid kit to clean and bandage the gash on my throat. The bone had pierced my skin where I thought I had stabbed the kushtaka's hand or paw.

I hoped I might have mortally wounded it. My research hadn't revealed exactly what dog bones did to kushtakas, so I had no way of knowing what would be effective. I had visions of driving the bone like a stake into my enemy's heart, as one supposedly did to a vampire. It made more sense than anything else, except maybe a stab between the eyes, a vision that gave me some small satisfaction since the horror of what I'd done to Sandra.

That vivid memory caused me a bad moment as I sat in a booth eating breakfast. A waitress hovered near, concerned. I explained weakly that my throat hurt. She brought a couple of aspirin, which I gratefully accepted. Shortly after that I paid and left, hoping to travel as far as possible in the available daylight.

I worried the authorities might be looking for me. Since I had booked the bedroom to Toronto, Sandra's body might not be found till then, but if a porter went in to change the bedding and discovered her, they could be searching for me already. Had using the emergency releases on the window set off an alarm? I imagined they would know everything about me from my credit card number.

I decided to move south and cross the border. The sooner I did that, perhaps the less likelihood of being caught by the police.

I hitchhiked again, with much better luck. I even managed to get a ride across the Canada/U.S. border into Montana. I faked a nap, assuring my host beforehand that I didn't carry anything illegal. The customs agent accepted the driver's word. She let us pass while I played opossum, listening tensely to the exchange. If the authorities sought me for the murder of Sandra Livingston, word hadn't yet reached this particular border crossing.

In my relief I lapsed into genuine sleep and didn't wake up until we reached Butte. I spent the night in a tool shed, then continued east for lack of a better direction.

It took me all day to get to the town of Big Timber, where I ate a hearty meal. Warmed and invigorated, I set a brisk pace along the road out of town rather than seeking a place to spend the night.

By the time I began to consider my situation realistically I had covered too much ground to justify returning to town. Pulling my jacket closer, I increased my pace, warily scanning the road ahead and behind me. The cool night in high country required a bit more warmth than my clothes or increased exercise could provide. I became dangerously cold.

Reluctantly I decided to stop, admitting the diminished chance of getting a ride in the dark. Choosing the top of a short grade for its view of the surrounding area, I left the road, crossed a drainage ditch, and selected a place to build a small fire.

The cold and my growing fear soon became numbing. If the kushtaka should happen upon me, I'd be completely exposed. Since it managed to find me at the abrupt end of my long train ride, I little doubted it could do so again.

I dozed a bit, but passed most of the night in dull half-consciousness.

Just before dawn, as my fire died, a low figure loped over a rise, heading in my direction, closing the gap at incredible speed. I gaped at the approaching animal. I knew it wasn't a coyote by the way it ran. It was a large timber wolf, extinct in this part of the state as far as I knew. When it was almost upon me, close enough to reveal eyes that glowed unnaturally red, I fumbled for my weapon and stumbled to my feet.

The wolf probably weighed close to a hundred pounds, and at a dead run it hit like a freight train, knocking me off my feet. Seizing my left arm in its powerful jaws, it jerked me along with it as its bulk passed over me. Landing with feet well planted, it immediately began to shake me roughly as I fought back.

To my amazement, I'd managed not to drop my weapon in the impact. I stabbed viciously, sinking the blade repeatedly into the wolf's throat and chest as it dragged me back and forth. Its breath blew hot in my face, spraying mixed saliva and blood. To my horror I seemed to feel the bones of my forearm grind together under its jaws as it bore down with its full weight.

We struggled nose-to-nose when the lupine features altered suddenly, becoming the face of the kushtaka. The red eyes burned, unchanged in the transformation, and it spoke guttural, unintelligible threats into the arm wedged in its teeth. The canines of a wolf sinking into my flesh unnerved me enough, but nothing compared to the sight of the dagger-like incisors of the kushtaka imbedded in my arm.

Inexplicably, in that instant my fear gave way to rage. I drove my weapon deeper into the beast's exposed ribs, twisting and yanking the blade in all directions.

Wolfish features returned as my weapon wrenched from my grasp. The animal released me to turn and bite at the blade lodged in its side. I grabbed my pack strap and swung, blindsiding the wolf and knocking it off my chest.

I scrambled to my feet, clambered across the ditch, and ran for my life. I realized suddenly that I'd left my sheath knife between the wolf's ribs, not the bone blade I'd prepared. That and my downhill path added momentum to my flight. My sides ached, my lungs felt seared, but I continued to run hard, concentrating on controlling my breathing, careful not to stumble.

I'd actually covered a fair distance when I heard a vehicle approaching from behind. In desperation I turned and stepped into the road, waving wildly. An old pickup truck pulled to a stop beside me. The driver, a weathered cowboy, regarded me calmly as I opened the door and leapt inside.

"Thanks," I panted, slamming the door. I collapsed against the seat, struggling to recover. The man began to drive on, but glanced in his rearview mirror and stopped.

"You forgot your dog," he said.

I twisted in the seat to look. The wolf ran down the grade toward us. I tried to speak but couldn't. I could only shake my head frantically.

"He can ride in the truck bed," he drawled, "it's no trouble." I grabbed his arm, fighting to form the words I needed to get us away from there. He looked down at my torn, bleeding wrist, took in my wild, dirty appearance, then shifted slightly in his seat.

His expression betrayed his thoughts. He had decided I was trouble, and intended to eject me from his truck.

I glanced back. The kushtaka was almost upon us. I gripped his arm tighter, staring into his eyes. My throat felt completely dry, my tongue dusty and swollen. As my head buzzed and I fought to form words an eternity seemed to pass—time we could not spare.

"Drive," I choked, "Danger." He looked hard at me, then quickly slammed the truck into gear and pulled onto the road, fishtailing in the gravel. Even as I turned to look back, a great weight hit the bed of the truck, shaking us.

"What the hell?" the man shouted. He looked over his shoulder. "What the *hell?*"

As he stared at the creature we nearly left the road, but he caught himself and corrected course with a yank of the wheel.

I ducked away as the kushtaka's hairy fist plunged through the cab window. The crook of a meaty arm engulfed the man's windpipe and jerked him bodily through the small opening, shattering the rest of the glass.

Without thinking I slid over on the seat, straightened the wheel, then jammed on the brakes. I held firm till the wheels began to lock, then stomped on the accelerator, shifting frantically.

I saw the kushtaka and its hapless victim tumble out the back of the truck, locked in a deadly embrace, then they were gone.

The rising sun cleared the horizon, momentarily distracting me from what had just happened. I slapped the sun visor down to block it, and drove.

I neared the limits of sanity. I could find no safe haven for my thoughts. Whenever my mind fled from the fantastic creature pursuing me it turned to the more believable danger of my situation. If I couldn't grasp the reality of this mythological beast, if that's what it was, or its unexplainable powers, I could certainly understand the consequences of murder and grand theft auto. These crimes were enough burden to bear without the additional weight of a pursuer from the unknown. It seemed only blind reaction had kept me alive and free to this point, and continued to be my only hope, dismal as that may be.

The road I traveled took me to a place called Harlowton. Outside of town I slowed until I found a dry wash. Driving the truck into the depression, I parked it by a clump of scrubby trees, satisfied they would screen it well enough from the road to conceal it for a while.

The morning had advanced by then, bolstering my remaining courage enough to allow a change into my last clean clothes before walking to town.

I found a beautiful stone hotel, standing like a fortress at the prairie's edge. Risking one more use of my credit card, I rented a room with a commanding view of the country I'd just traveled.

In privacy I bathed my torn arm and carefully bandaged it with a towel. I tried to sleep, but my fear-honed senses alerted me to every sound—the low conversation of other guests, the clink of silverware in the cafe downstairs, laughter from the saloon. In the late afternoon I gave up the effort, bought a bottle of tequila, and began my vigil.

♦ ♦ ♦ ♦ ♦

This room has become my only reality. If I doubt it, I need only rap my forehead smartly on the tabletop toward which it droops to reassure myself.

I'm so tired.

My thoughts wander from the events that led me here to the many questions about the strange creature. My curiosity has come to haunt me almost as much as the thing itself. What compels it to pursue me so tenaciously, even to the point of straying so incredibly far from its homeland—our homeland? I search my memory for any clue. Had I broken some taboo in Thomas Bay? Had I personally offended the beast somehow, causing it to track me all these miles?

What is the thing, really? I find that I crave confirmation of its identity. Is it the legendary kushtaka, the gageets? Does a long-overlooked zoological text somewhere in the world contain a scientific description of it? I would almost offer myself up to its deadly purpose if it would only take a moment beforehand to tell me about itself. Such curiosity is ridiculous, of course, almost obsessive, but after all, it appears I have very little else for which to live.

My thoughts return to Sandra. I grieve for her, stricken by the knowledge I had killed her, had drained the blood from those soft, warm lips, and stopped her heart. I took away her life, when all I ever wanted to do was give her mine.

Her memory haunts me, too. We had been so good together for so long. I ache to realize it really was her on the train, and I had read the signals right. For whatever reason, she wanted to reconcile, but I killed her because I thought she was the kushtaka.

How I wish I could have those critical moments back. If only she were still alive. If only she were here....

I sense her at the door of my little hotel room. I see the knob turn under her gentle hand, anticipating the touch of that hand on my skin, the whisper of her breath on the nape of my neck. I see her stand before me, radiant, with warm, loving eyes, red hair, and her sweet, sweet smile.

"Why, Darling—what big teeth you have!"

STORY NOTES

SHY GHOSTS DANCING: In 1993 my sister, Beth, and I canoed from Juneau to Admiralty Island to camp for a few days on the beach near Bear Creek. We explored the creek during a salmon run, coming into close contact with, although never actually seeing the island's brown bears. While there we enjoyed spectacular, almost nightly aurora borealis displays. This is one of the few times I've actually seen the aurora *before* sunset. One night I made the shy ghost comment attributed to Dora in the story. The rest of the tale grew from there, and draws much of its ambient detail from our adventure on the island.

I found it challenging to cast brown bears as a dangerous element in this story while staying true to their behavior. The relationship between bears and humans is extremely complex. While perfectly capable of extreme, horrific violence, bears are almost always peaceful toward humans, wanting only to be left alone. Imagine living near a powerfully strong, reclusive, grumpy, yet loving uncle who also happens to be a homicidal schizophrenic—he'll most likely never hurt you, but you must always be prepared for the eventuality. Respect is the proper attitude. For every gruesome bear attack, there are dozens of encounters in which bears have been gentle, mildly curious, even playful or nurturing! All of my extremely few bear encounters have been comical. I hope that remains true throughout my life.

An editor who considered this story felt that I had "betrayed" the reader by shifting points of view in the final paragraphs. I don't believe betrayal has ever been among my many motives for writing—and I sincerely hope that you don't feel betrayed by this choice.

WHACKING THE GROANER: As a boy in Sitka, Alaska, the whistle buoy or "groaner" somewhere out in the sound below the house contributed to the soundtrack of my life. That life has always included a love for dinosaurs and other prehistoric creatures, so a marriage of the two seemed inevitable.

Long after I wrote this tale, I read Ray Bradbury's 1951 short story, *The Fog Horn*. I'm sure I didn't read it before writing *Whacking the Groaner*. It looks like I stole the idea, but that isn't the case. Honest.

THE BLOOFER LADY: I love Bram Stoker's *Dracula*, especially for the many subtle textures of the story, many of which never seem to appeal to the many filmmakers who have used and abused the original material. When Lucy Westenra becomes vampiric, a child in the area complains of attacks by "the Bloofer Lady." Stoker mentions this almost in passing, with no explanation of the term. It has always piqued my imagination.

When we visit recreational cabins around Southeast Alaska, reading the logbook is always a major source of entertainment. I liked the idea of sitting alone in one of these cabins in the middle of nowhere, reading a tale of horror played out in journal form. The device also allows me to distance the reader from the story's victim, restricting access to his more subtle thoughts and impressions. The result leaves our information sketchy, raising unanswered questions. Alaskans are very familiar with this feeling, as mysterious disappearances, accidents, and deaths here often leave us at the same disadvantage in trying to discern what happened.

This story also owes much to my father's kushtaka story (below) and Stephen Grendon's excellent short story, *The Drifting Snow*.

THE CONSERVER: Work on a project over time, then leave it alone for a few years, and you'll inevitably find a few surprises when you eventually return to it. I started this story as a vignette, perhaps with a notion of incorporating it into a novel. When I began pulling together material for this book, I checked all the unfinished works I've accumulated over the years. I realized that this one, at least, could be considered complete as it is.

I find the story very ironic, considering that I wrote it while working for a massive bureaucracy in a larger Alaskan "city." To read it now, sitting at my table in a remote, off-the-grid cabin, seems to be fulfilling destiny on a certain level.

THE FEAR: This might be the oldest story in this collection. I'm no longer certain how long ago I wrote it; I finished it in 1993, but probably began writing it before 1990. See more in notes on *Ghost Wanted* below.

The primary inspiration for the story is a dream I had, which was exactly as described in the story. The rest, other than the primary action, is largely autobiographical. An earlier draft included a description of my experience seeing the film *Jaws* for the first time. We were in Ketchikan, Alaska for a regional school event. My peers made up most of the theater audience, all of us children of maritime communities, which made it an almost tribal event, an orgy of fear that I'll never forget!

Do I really have "The Fear?" No. I don't know why. I did have almost all of the thoughts and feelings described in the story once, but other cares and concerns have far outweighed them, I guess.

THE CRY OF A LOON: This story more than any of the others here comes close to expressing the mysterious atmosphere of Southeast Alaska to my satisfaction. A key element of the story is so personal that when a magazine editor commented that he doubted that it was at all credible (when, in fact, I'd lifted it directly from my personal experience) I shelved the story for years. Writing wisdom says, "Write what you know." It doesn't say what to do if no one believes what you know!

I used parts of the story in several others included here, but when I decided to self publish, I realized that I could present the story to the public if I wanted, editor's doubts notwithstanding. I pulled the elements back in, dusted it off, and include it here for your enjoyment.

GHOST WANTED: If not *The Fear*, then this is the oldest story in this collection. I transcribed it onto a computer from typewritten pages in 1993, but I don't remember how long I'd carried that manuscript around.

I may have written it before finding the courage to write specifically about my Alaskan life. Or, I might have shied away from doing so in this story, having used so much autobiographical material in *The Fear*. The true sequence is lost to me now.

Some of the practical jokes attributed here to Alan were real pranks that have been described to me by others, including the witch silhouette that appeared on an opera's moonset lighting effect during a Halloween performance. On a different night, the chain drive used to lower the same moon jammed, so that the luminous disk stalled briefly before suddenly dropping from sight!

Raven's Tale Magazine accepted this story for publication, but folded before it appeared in print.

LONG BLACK VEIL: This may be the newest story in this collection. I drew inspiration, point of view, and tense from the folk song of the same name, and from the dramatic masks of Hokhokw, the mythical cannibal bird of the Kwakwaka'wak (Kwakiutl) nation of Canada.

I aspired to present this story in an older style reminiscent of Edgar Allan Poe and H.P. Lovecraft that has perhaps fallen out of fashion. I hope that it doesn't come off as stilted in the current age.

WHISPERS IN THE TREES: I once participated in a theater project in Juneau in which we used the ruins of a mining town as our theater and stage. When we chose pieces to perform, I wanted to submit my own work to be performed, but my stories were all too long. I wrote this very short story to submit instead. It didn't make the cut.

At the time, I'd shelved *The Cry of a Loon*, so I used its setting as inspiration, and borrowed many of my favorite passages from it as well. Once I decided to publish the older story, I had to delete those passages from this story. I found that it still worked fairly well; I hope you agree.

SHELIKOF BAY: This might be my favorite story here. I have always loved the selkie and roan legends of my Celtic ancestors. It seems natural for me to marry them (if you will) and the regions from which they originated with the outer coast of Southeast Alaska. Also mixed in are my magical memories of a family vacation at the U.S. Forest Service cabin in Shelikof Bay when I was a child.

The end of the story can be seen coming from the first few lines; there's not much in the way of suspense here. Hopefully, the value lies in the telling, not the tale—hopefully, it's not the arriving that matters, but the journey itself.

Ironically, I submitted this story to a small press magazine that specialized in mythology-based fiction. They rejected it because it was too much like the film, *The Secret of Roan Inish*. Since both works explicitly refer to the same myths and legends, there would naturally be similarities! They say one should never talk back to editors, but I question the quality of a magazine that claims mythological traditions as its theme, yet cannot, in fact, recognize those traditions when they appear!

MOTHER IS A SELKIE: Placed here as a companion piece to *Shelikof Bay*, this poem used to be the opening lines of that story, which also shared the poem's title. I eventually cut it to preserve what little suspense the piece might otherwise hold, but I included it here as an interlude of sorts.

CHILDREN OF THE FOREST: I got the title of this piece from an apparently true story about a missionary who preached to a congregation of northwest coast Natives through an interpreter. He addressed them poetically, if patronizingly, as "children of the forest." Unfortunately, the translator interpreted that as "little people stationed among the sticks," which did not go over well. The two phrases melded in my mind to create the wholly imaginary race of beings described in the story.

MORLEY'S DREAM: I have long had a favorite recurring dream somewhat similar to Morley's, but without the personal involvement in the shop (it's usually a museum in my dream). This story is my attempt to describe aspects of it.

NONE BUT THE DEAD: The habit of "collecting" from "abandoned" Native villages while the residents were away at fish camp is well documented on the Northwest Coast. Call this a revenge fantasy, if you will.

Writing from Hedricksen's point of view required me to use terms and reflect attitudes that contradict the way I was raised. That wasn't easy! Referring to First Nations People as "Indians" was hard; even the term "totem sticks," common in that era, sets my teeth on edge! Stand next to even the humblest totem pole, look up at it, and call it a "stick." Go on, I dare you.... Such impressive, massive works of art are not sticks!

This is the most explicitly erotic story I've ever tried to present to the public. I'm always torn between expressing myself and fear of offending, but I guess the proper response to that is best left up to the reader.

THE RAVEN CALLS AT DAWN: For a white man to write a story about a Native "legend" is a perilous undertaking, particularly here on the northwest Pacific coast, where Native cultures regard stories as private property. I have great respect for these nations, among which I was raised, and do not mean to violate their customs and sensibilities in any way, in this or any of my stories that draw upon their rich heritage.

Stories of the kushtaka, it might be argued, have spread beyond "legend" to permeate all of Southeast Alaskan culture. (I quote the terms "legend" or "myth" in this context, because I am reluctant to so quickly dismiss or trivialize a being, force, or phenomenon that has had such profound affect on so many people, some of whom I know and respect.) Stories, rumors, and, in some cases, a good deal of lying about this mysterious being abound here, as indicated by J. Robert Alley's *Raincoast Sasquatch* (Hancock House Publishers, 2003) and Harry D. Colp's *The Strangest Story Ever Told* (Pilot Publishing, Inc., 1994).

My personal introduction to kushtakas came from a story my father told me shortly before the family returned to Alaska in the late '60s. I remember it being very similar to Colp's story. Dad might have paraphrased it. His descriptions and imagery both terrified and enchanted me. A few years later in Sitka I saw Chuck D. Keen's film, *Joniko and the Kush Ta Ka,* and continued to hear stories, rumors, and firsthand accounts of experiences with the unknown creature. I have even had a personal experience in Thomas Bay that, while it would be a stretch to blame it on kushtakas, could be construed as mysterious and perhaps even sinister.

The Raven Calls at Dawn draws on all of these sources, and takes them to extremes for my own satisfaction. I must therefore stress that *this story should not be regarded as a reliable source of kushtaka lore!* If I've piqued your interest in the subject, please search out the stories and legends from original sources. You'll soon discern the liberties I've taken.

I'm struck by the similarities in the relationship between Native cultures and kushtakas, and the relationship my Celtic ancestors have to the Fair Folk (fairies). Both may be regarded with great fear, yet both can be beneficial or deadly, at their whim. They are like Nature personified, unpredictably good, bad, or indifferent depending on the circumstance. Living each day as we do on the homestead in and as a part of Nature, this notion appeals to me greatly. Viewing the "legend" in this light, I feel I have done the kushtaka an injustice, wrenching it from the source and seat of its power to send it across the country in pursuit of one insignificant human.

Certain less fantastic elements of this story come directly from my life. The descriptions of the blind bird living in the totem pole, and the pack dynamics of the local dogs come from my wife, Michelle's and my personal experiences in the village of Gitwangak, British Columbia, Canada. The local, semi-feral dogs "adopted" Michelle much as described. When I approached her, they closed ranks around her and warned me off! After she let them know I was not a threat, they became friendly to me as well.

The reference to the mother's pet pig and its demise comes from my mother's childhood experience.

Shapeshifter! Magazine (the Stygian Vortex publication, not the bodybuilding magazine that goes by that name today) published this piece in 1995 in what I believe was their only issue. That makes this the one story I ever sold. They edited me so gently, they changed one single word! I was far less lenient in preparing it for publication here, and I believe the story's much improved for it.

AFTERWORD

The tales collected here vastly exaggerate much of what there is to fear in the Alaskan wilderness. It is, indeed, a dangerous place. There are, in fact, many mysterious unknowns to be found here. And yet, people live here happily in varying relationships with, and attitudes toward The Wild. Like anyplace else, death and danger take myriad forms here, often mundane, even trivial. Perhaps what makes Alaska different is its scope—the mystery, like the state itself, is writ large.

In delving into my past as I collected and prepared these stories, I've questioned my own relationship to Alaska. I've changed somewhat from the man who wrote most of these stories while living in a suburb of the state's third largest city (a large town by "lower 48" standards). It's not that I fear The Wild less having moved into it, because I only ever feared it in the archaic sense of the term, meaning to hold it in proper awe and respect. That has not changed.

Perhaps what has changed is my relationship to that mysterious quality I discussed in the foreword. I still get caught up in it, but I have also discovered that I am often a part of it now. I have watched people and animals stare steadfastly at an object, vainly trying to divine its true shape and identity from its appearance alone, only to discover (belatedly, sometimes) that *I* am that object.

But don't take my word for it—come and see Alaska for yourself!

ACKNOWLEDGMENTS

My heartfelt thanks to the following:

My late mother, Gertie Zeiger, who edited my first story for publication without benefit of college education or formal experience, just her innate intelligence and common sense. She saw that first one published; I wish she'd lived to see this book. She believed in me, and taught me to believe in myself.

My father, Bill Zeiger, who told me stories, and whose willingness to live and work in Alaska led to my birth in "The Great Land."

My stepmother, Nada Zeiger, for her understanding and encouragement.

My beloved siblings: My younger sister, Beth, who camped with me on *Kootznoowoo*, over which the shy ghosts danced, and our older brother, David, who provided so much material for these stories, and who asked the key question that led to this book. Thank you both for your love, companionship, and laughter, for encouraging this book, and for everything. And, thanks, David, for teaching me the futility of throwing a punch while treading water.

My father-in-law and poet, Richard Lee Harris, for showing me it could be done.

All the Tlingit and Haida elders, especially Robert Zuboff and A.P. Johnson, who shared their stories with me and others through the years.

Haines author, "frontier rhetorician," and friend Daniel Henry for his support, enthusiasm, and knowledge.

The editors and staffs of *Shapeshifter! Magazine* (Stygian Vortex Productions) and *Raven's Tale* for publishing and intending to publish my stories.

To Edward L. Keithahn, for his wonderful book, *Monuments in Cedar* (Superior Publishing Company, 1958) that fired the imagination of a small Alaskan boy.

The enthusiastic readers of our blog at AKZeigers.com.

Most especially to my loving, patient wife, Michelle, who has believed in me for so long. And our precious daughter, Aly, my infant muse when I wrote these stories, my partner in adventure, who then and now makes me feel like I could be the father she believes me to be.

ABOUT THE AUTHOR

Mark Zeiger has lived in Alaska, his native state, for most of his life. He now lives a mostly subsistence lifestyle on his semi-remote, off-the-grid homestead on the shore of Lynn Canal, south of Haines. He designs Websites and blogs about his family's homestead life at AKZeigers.com. He's currently working on a memoir of homestead living and other books. He lives with his wife, Michelle, their daughter, Aly, and their cat, Spice.

The electricity used to write, edit, design and illustrate *Shy Ghosts Dancing: Dark Tales from Southeast Alaska* came exclusively from alternative sources—wind and solar power generated on the Zeiger's off-the-grid homestead.